The Secret of the Island Treasure

In the earthen chamber under the treasure pit, Joe crouched next to Bill and studied the hole in the wall by the light of the lantern.

"It looks like some kind of tunnel," Joe called up to Frank. "You know, this may sound crazy, but I think I hear gurgling water inside it."

"Yeah," said Bill. "I hear it, too."

"Maybe you've discovered some pirate plumbing," Frank suggested. "A drinking fountain for thirsty treasure buriers."

"It's getting louder," said Joe, putting his ear to the hole. "It's almost like the water's coming toward us."

"Let's get out of here!" cried Bill, suddenly panicked.

"It's only a little water," scoffed Joe. "Are you afraid to get—"

All at once a thick column of water burst out of the hole, hitting Joe so hard it knocked him against the far wall of the chamber. As Frank watched, helpless, Joe slumped to the ground.

The Hardy Boys Mystery Stories

Available from MINSTREL Books

100

The HARDY BOYS®

THE SECRET OF THE ISLAND TREASURE

FRANKLIN W. DIXON

A MINSTREL® BOOK

PUBLISHED BY POCKET BOOKS

New York   London   Toronto   Sydney   Tokyo   Singapore

A MINSTREL PAPERBACK *ORIGINAL*

A Minstrel Book published by
POCKET BOOKS, a division of Simon & Schuster Inc.
1230 Avenue of the Americas, New York, NY 10020

Copyright © 1990 by Simon & Schuster Inc.
Cover art copyright © 1990 by Paul Bachem
Produced by Mega-Books of New York, Inc.

ISBN: 0-671-69450-2

First Minstrel Books printing February 1990

10 9 8 7 6 5 4 3 2

THE HARDY BOYS MYSTERY STORIES is a trademark of Simon & Schuster Inc.

THE HARDY BOYS, A MINSTREL BOOK and colophon are registered trademarks of Simon & Schuster Inc.

Printed in the U.S.A.

Contents

THE SECRET
OF THE ISLAND
TREASURE

1 Tower Secret

"Somebody give me some suspenseful music," said eighteen-year-old Frank Hardy, as he drove his modified, dark blue police van down a tree-lined road on the outskirts of Bayport. "We're almost there."

"*Dum* dum *dum dum*," sang his seventeen-year-old blond-haired brother, Joe. He was in the passenger seat, squinting his blue eyes out the open window.

"*Dum* de *dum dum*," added the Hardys' friend Chet Morton. "*Dum* de *dum dum dummmmmm!*"

"As the camera tracks slowly down the deserted country road," said Frank in the smooth voice of a TV newscaster, "we suddenly see gloomy old Tower Mansion looming like an ancient fortress over the town of Bayport."

"And there it is!" said Joe, pointing through a clearing in the trees. The huge old mansion glowered down at them from the top of a low hill. It was two stories tall, built of stone, and flanked by a pair of towers that looked as though they'd been stolen from a medieval castle. The house cast a long and eerie shadow in the morning sunlight.

Chet shivered slightly. "This place is totally creepy. And the closer we get, the creepier it looks."

"Come on, Chet, it's not that bad," Frank said. "The mansion is kind of neat. Spooky but neat."

Frank pulled the Hardy van into the mansion's driveway and parked it next to an old foreign-made car. The three teens climbed out of the van and stared up at the mansion.

"Brings back memories, doesn't it?" Joe said to his brother.

"Definitely," Frank said, his brown eyes twinkling. He felt a thrill of excitement as he remembered how he and his brother had solved their first case as detectives here at the mansion. Well, not exactly at the mansion. They had been searching for stolen money hidden in one of the mansion's towers. But the money had actually been concealed in an old water tower near the railroad tracks. Still, one of the most important figures in the case had been old Hurd Applegate, who owned the mansion and lived there with his sister, Adelia.

2

"I can't believe that the Applegates decided to sell this place," said Joe.

"What I can't believe," said Frank, "is that the developer who bought it is going to turn it into condominiums."

"Condos?" said Chet, looking up at the house. "Who'd want to live here? Count Dracula?"

A second van, battered and covered with dried flecks of paint, turned into the driveway and parked behind the Hardys' van. A trio of burly workmen, wearing overalls, climbed out and glanced briefly at Frank, Joe, and Chet. Then they opened up the back of the van and began pulling out equipment. One of them glanced at the three teens again as he puffed on a fat cigar, then turned back to his companions. Their arms filled with ladders and buckets of paint, the workmen headed up the driveway to the mansion.

"They must work for the developer who bought the mansion," said Frank.

"Do you think Mr. Applegate and his sister will live in one of the condos?" Joe asked.

"There's only one way to find out," said Frank. "Let's go."

The three friends started up the driveway to the old mansion. As they approached the front door they saw a tall older man in a faded black suit that had gone out of style years before. The man was

3

standing in the entryway, angrily waving a cane at the three workmen.

"There's Hurd Applegate," said Joe. "And he doesn't look too happy."

The workmen finally stepped past Hurd and headed through the front door of the mansion, ladders and cans of paint in hand. Hurd glared at them, then turned back to the front yard. As his eyes fell on Frank and Joe and their companion, his expression changed to a bright smile and he stood up straighter.

"Well, as I live and breathe!" he said. "It's the young Hardy brothers, Frank and Joe."

"Hello, Mr. Applegate," said Frank, strolling up the front walkway.

"It's good to see you, Mr. Applegate," said Joe, following his brother. "And this is Chet Morton. You remember him, don't you?"

"Of course. Wonderful to see you!" Hurd Applegate pumped Chet's hand. "What brings you boys here today?"

"We heard you were selling the mansion," said Frank, "and that it's being turned into condos. We wanted to see for ourselves if the rumors were true."

"Judging from those workmen we just saw come up the walk," said Joe, "the rumors *must* be true."

At the mention of the workmen, Hurd's face clouded over. "Those louts," he snarled. "Always

4

acting disrespectful, flicking cigar ashes around the mansion, tracking paint all over the place—"

"What about the mansion?" Frank put in quickly.

"Ah, yes," said Hurd, his face brightening. "It's all true, everything you've heard. I've sold the mansion to Vernon Prescott of Prescott Enterprises. And yes, he's converting it into condominiums. Got a pretty penny for it, too!"

"But why did you sell it?" asked Frank. "The Tower Mansion is a Bayport landmark."

"They won't be tearing it down," Hurd explained. "And I won't be moving out. My sister, Adelia, and I have kept our own apartments here. Adelia's is in the new tower, and mine is in the old. We're not young people anymore, you know."

"How is Miss Applegate doing?" Joe asked.

"Adelia's just fine. Come on in, boys," Hurd said, waving them past him. "I'm sure she'll be glad to see you."

Hurd closed the heavily carved oak door and led his visitors inside. The foyer of the mansion was spacious and high-ceilinged. In the middle of the room, a broad staircase rose toward the upper floor of the mansion. The room would have looked very elegant if it hadn't been for the grayish white dropcloths draped over the floor and the furniture.

"Adelia!" shouted Hurd. "We have guests!"

A handsome elderly woman appeared from another room. Her faded blond hair was tied behind

5

her head, and she wore a purple caftan cinched at the waist with an orange sash so bright that it hurt to look at it. Frank, Joe, and Chet smiled, remembering Adelia's unusual taste in clothes. The woman stared at the teens for a moment, then grinned.

"You're the young men who helped Hurd retrieve his money!" she exclaimed. "How nice of you to stop by and see us."

"Frank and Joe Hardy," Hurd reminded her. "And their friend Chet Morton. They've come to see how we're doing."

"Then you must have some tea with us," Adelia announced. "You *can* stay for a while, can't you?"

"For a few minutes, anyway," Frank said.

"But first," said Hurd, "I want you to see my apartment. My very own condominium. I'm so excited about it. The workers should be there now. Come with me, boys. It's in the old tower."

"The old tower?" asked Chet nervously. "Are you sure we want to go up there, guys?"

"Why not?" asked Joe with a grin. "Afraid you won't survive the climb?"

"I've heard that the old tower's haunted," said Chet. "The first owner kept someone in a secret dungeon up there. The prisoner died and now his ghost haunts the place."

"My father, Major Applegate, was the first owner of the mansion," Hurd snapped, "and he did *not* keep prisoners in the tower. I can assure you of that."

Frank gave Chet a hard look. "You'll have to excuse Chet, Mr. Applegate," he said. "He has an overactive imagination."

"Hey," said Chet, holding up his hands. "I was just repeating what I heard, okay?"

"Well, next time, keep it to yourself," Joe said.

"Follow me," said Hurd, starting briskly up the staircase. "Believe me, if there were any ghosts in this tower, I'm sure I would have seen them by now."

He led them up to a wide landing on the second floor. Joe looked around, remembering the time he and Frank had searched the place fruitlessly for hours, trying to find the missing money. When he caught Frank looking around, too, the Hardys exchanged glances and laughed.

They followed Hurd down a series of corridors to a spiral staircase in the northeast corner of the mansion, which led directly into one of the towers. After climbing another four floors, they came to a narrow landing with a single window looking out on the wide body of water that was Barmet Bay.

"That was a real climb," said Frank. "Are you sure you want to walk up all those stairs every day, Mr. Applegate?"

"I'll have you know that I'm in fine physical

condition," Hurd replied sharply. "In any case, Vernon Prescott will be putting a small elevator in each tower."

Hurd led them down the hall and through an open door. The room inside was small compared to some of the other rooms in the mansion, but a picture window looked out over the bay. Another door led into another room. Opposite the window was a blank wall. The three workmen were already in the room, hard at work tearing off old wallpaper and priming the wall underneath.

"That's some view," said Chet, staring out the window. "You can really see how big the bay is. And you can see islands in it and everything."

"Hey, you're right," said Joe, standing beside Chet and looking out. "This is fantastic!"

The workman with the cigar gave Joe a dirty look, as if he were annoyed at having his work interrupted. Then he turned back to what he had been doing: driving a nail into the wall. The sound of his hammer echoed loudly in the small room.

"This will be a great apartment when it's finished," said Frank. "Thanks for showing it to us, Mr. Ap—"

A loud ripping noise interrupted Frank in midsentence. He turned to see the cigar-smoking workman stumble backward as the wall he had been hammering on suddenly caved in. A large slab of wood fell to the floor with a thud, leaving behind a gaping hole in the middle of the wall.

Hurd Applegate's eyes flashed angrily. "What have you done now?" he snapped.

"Don't blame me!" the workman shouted defensively. "That old wood's just rotten. It fell apart when I hit it."

A second workman grabbed the edge of the hole and peered inside. "Hey, look at this!" he said. "There's another room in here."

"The secret dungeon!" Chet said with a moan.

"Take it easy, Chet," said Joe. "It's probably just an old closet somebody boarded up and forgot about."

"No," Hurd Applegate said quietly. "It must be my father's secret workroom. He died when I was a young boy. I used to hear rumors about the room from men who worked with my father, but I've never been able to find it. I thought it didn't exist."

"Wow," murmured Joe. "A secret workroom!"

"Open it up!" commanded Hurd, waving his cane at the workmen.

Wordlessly, the men began to rip at the wall with hammers and crowbars, until there was a hole large enough to enter through. One of the workers pulled a flashlight from his toolbox and aimed it inside. Spider webs glittered in the beam of light, hiding much of the room from view.

"Who wants to go first?" the workman asked.

"Give me that flashlight!" Hurd snapped. He plucked the flashlight from the workman's hands. "You workmen stay out here," he ordered. "This is private. Frank, Joe, Chet, you follow me." He stepped cautiously through the hole in the wall and into the darkness beyond, sweeping spider webs aside with his hand.

The workman who had held the flashlight shrugged. Then he and the other two men began to strip off wallpaper again.

Frank, Joe, and Chet followed after Hurd. The small room was dark and dusty. Hurd swung the flashlight beam in slow circles, revealing shelves lined with books and file folders, old wooden cabinets full of drawers, and an antique rolltop desk with papers stacked high on top of it.

"This is incredible," said Hurd. "My father's papers. His books. I thought they were lost forever."

"I guess we didn't search this place as carefully as we thought the last time we were here," said Frank. "We missed a whole room."

"Hey, what's that?" said Chet, as the beam of the flashlight revealed a sheet of yellowing parchment next to some papers on top of the desk. "It looks like some kind of map."

"Don't touch that!" Hurd ordered. "Old papers are delicate. You might destroy it."

10

"It *is* a map," said Frank, picking the paper up carefully. "It looks like a really old map of Barmet Bay."

"Right," said Joe. "It's old, but you can tell it's Bayport." He touched a spot on the map with his finger. "See? There's Lookout Hill."

"What's this?" said Chet, pointing to a bright red X marking the spot where Barmet Bay emptied into the Atlantic Ocean. "Looks like something important."

"Let me see that!" demanded Hurd, elbowing Chet aside and focusing the flashlight beam on the old piece of parchment. He stared at the paper and shook his head slowly. "I'd heard of this map, but I never believed . . ."

He looked down at the spot on the map where Chet had been pointing, next to the red X. A silence fell over the entire room.

Next to the X, clearly marked on the map of Barmet Bay, was a single word:

"Treasure"!

2 Granite Cay

Joe stared at the map in disbelief. "Treasure?" he asked quietly. "Does it mean, you know, *treasure?*"

"I think that's what it means, yeah," said Frank. "You always did have a way with words."

"Do you think this could be some kind of pirate map?" asked Chet.

"Possibly," said Hurd, taking the map from Frank. "But the word *treasure* is in my father's handwriting."

"What sort of treasure do you think it is?" asked Joe. "Gold? Jewels? Old Spanish doubloons?"

"It doesn't say on the map," said Hurd, staring at the markings on the sheet of paper.

"How do we know we can even find this treasure?" asked Frank. "The X on the map is in the middle of Barmet Bay. The treasure could be underwater."

"No way," said Joe, staring at the map over Hurd's shoulder. "There's some kind of island there. I can't make out the name."

"Granite Cay," Hurd Applegate said slowly, as though the name meant something to him but he couldn't remember what. "Granite Cay."

"That's what it says, all right," said Joe. "Granite Cay. Any of you guys ever heard of it?"

"Not me," said Chet.

"Me, neither," said Frank.

"Mr. Applegate?"

Hurd turned the map over. On the back was an enlarged view of an island that was marked *Granite Cay*. Another bright red *X* marked a spot on the island. Everyone crowded around Hurd to get a closer look at the map of the island.

"This is great!" said Joe. "Just like one of those old pirate movies."

"You don't think the treasure's still there, do you?" asked Frank. "I mean, somebody's probably dug it up by now."

"Yeah, Major Applegate probably dug it up himself," said Joe.

"No," muttered Hurd, staring intently at the map. "If he had, Adelia and I would have heard about it."

"Mr. Applegate?" said Frank, noticing that the older man was looking at the map as if he were hypnotized. "Are you okay?"

"Granite Cay," Hurd muttered again. Suddenly his eyes lit up. "Granite Cay! Of course! Now I remember where I've heard the name before. My father *owned* the island."

"If your father owned the island," Chet said excitedly, "then *you* must own the island—and you can dig up the treasure! Er . . . you *do* still own the island, don't you, Mr. Applegate?"

"I'm not sure," said Hurd. "My father may have sold it. But if I still do, then the deed must be in this room somewhere!"

Frank looked around at the thick piles of paper that filled the room. "Great," he said, frowning. "It shouldn't take more than a decade or so to find it."

"Then we'd better start looking now," said Hurd, pawing through the papers on the desk.

"Have you heard about this treasure before, Mr. Applegate?" asked Joe.

"Yes," Hurd said distractedly. "It was one of the rumors that I'd heard. My father never talked about such things, but other people told me stories. They said he had searched for old pirate treasure but that he had never found it."

"If that map is accurate," said Frank, "he must have found out where the treasure was."

"I wonder why he never dug it up," said Joe.

"I have no idea," said Hurd shortly. "Here. Help me find the deed. Frank, you look in the papers on that shelf. Joe, look through these manila folders."

"We need some more light in here," said Frank. "There's only one flashlight, and I can hardly see. Maybe the workmen have another flashlight."

He stepped out of the secret room. As he did, he saw the last of the workmen slip out into the hallway, closing the door to the room behind him.

"Pretty short workday," Frank murmured. He reentered the secret room and told the others that the workmen had left.

"So much for a second flashlight," said Joe. "Chet, why don't you pull some of those boards loose to let more sunlight in?"

"That's right. Leave me to do the tough work," Chet said jokingly.

He grabbed the crowbar left behind by the workmen and began pulling boards loose from the wall. Rays of sunlight poured in, illuminating the dark corners of the narrow room.

"What does this deed look like?" asked Frank. "Just an old sheet of paper?"

"It should mention the name Granite Cay on the front of it," Hurd said. "And it should have my father's signature on it and some kind of official seal. It would be more than half a century old, so it should be turning yellow."

15

"Everything in this place is turning yellow," said Joe. "Including me, from all this dust."

Frank, Joe, and Hurd began shuffling systematically through the large piles of yellowing papers, searching for the deed. After Chet finished removing the boards from the wall, he took the flashlight and searched through the drawers and shelves. A half-hour later the four of them were still searching. There was no sign of the deed for Granite Cay.

Frank turned over the bottom paper in the stack through which he was searching. "Sorry, Mr. Applegate," he announced. "Nothing here."

"Here's something," said Joe, pulling a sheet of yellowing paper from a manila folder. "I don't think it's a deed, but it mentions Granite Cay and Major Applegate."

"Let me see that," said Hurd. Joe handed him the paper, and Hurd smoothed it out on the surface of the desk.

"It looks like a receipt," Hurd said. His eyes opened wider. "Oh, no! It's a bill of sale! It says that my father sold Granite Cay to someone else! I was afraid this might have happened!"

"But why would he sell the island if it had treasure on it?" Frank asked.

"He probably had no choice," said Hurd dismally. "My father was once on the brink of bankruptcy. No doubt if he hadn't sold the island, he might have lost his entire estate, even Tower Mansion. By the time he found the map, he probably couldn't afford to keep chasing after the elusive treasure." Hurd shook his head sadly.

"Who did he sell the island to?" asked Frank. "Maybe you can buy it back with the money you got for selling Tower Mansion."

Hurd's face brightened. "That's not a bad idea, young man. Let's see . . . the name on this deed is—Barrett Kingsley, I believe."

"Isn't there a Kingsley who runs a real-estate firm in town?" asked Frank. "I've seen his name in the paper."

"Oh, right," said Joe. "Barrett Kingsley the Third. He's the guy who built Bayport Mall."

"He must be the grandson of the original Barrett Kingsley," said Chet.

"Ah, yes," said Hurd. "*That* Kingsley. I considered selling Tower Mansion to him. Owns much of the land around Bayport, I hear."

"Then he probably still owns Granite Cay," said Joe.

"And I bet he owns so much that he doesn't even *know* that he owns Granite Cay," added Frank.

"I'll wager he doesn't know that it has treasure on it," said Hurd. "And I won't be the one to tell him." He looked at the Hardys and Chet. "Would you be willing to drive me to see Mr. Kingsley right away?"

17

"Sure," said Frank. "But is it really fair not to tell him about the treasure?"

"Yeah," said Joe. "It will sound like you're trying to run some kind of scam on him."

"That's *my* worry," said Hurd. "Just leave the negotiations to me. I'll take care of the details."

Frank and Joe exchanged doubting glances as Hurd exited from the room, the aging bill of sale in hand.

"Well," said Hurd, looking back over his shoulder at the Hardys and Chet. "What are you waiting for? Come on!"

Hurd ushered them back into the stairwell, then locked the outer door to his apartment. The group hurried down the stairs, the Hardys and Chet having trouble keeping up with the remarkably spry older man.

Adelia Applegate was waiting for them in the foyer with a tray of tea and biscuits, but Hurd waved her aside and announced that they were on their way to town on important business. Frank and Joe apologized to her for their hasty exit, then hurried through the front door after Hurd.

Hurd climbed into the passenger seat of the Hardys' van, Frank into the driver's seat, and Joe and Chet into the rear. Fifteen minutes later, they pulled up next to a large building in downtown Bayport. Carved over the front entrance were the words *The Kingsley Building*.

18

The building was lavishly decorated inside, with gold-trimmed lighting fixtures and wall-to-wall carpeting in the corridors. The elevator was large enough to hold about twenty-five people without crowding.

"This would make a nice rec room," said Joe, looking around as the elevator glided up to the twentieth floor.

"Or a basketball court," suggested Frank. "We could put the hoop over there."

When Hurd, Chet, and the Hardys stepped out of the elevator, they found themselves facing a severely dressed receptionist seated behind a rosewood-and-chrome desk.

"I want to speak to Mr. Kingsley!" Hurd announced loudly, waving his cane in the receptionist's face.

"You—you can't speak to him now," she stammered, a startled look in her eyes. "He's in a meeting. An important meeting."

"I'll speak to him whenever I please," snapped Hurd. "Tell Mr. Kingsley that Hurd Applegate is on his way into his office to conduct an important business transaction!"

"But—but—you can't—" the receptionist protested.

"Come with me, boys," said Hurd, setting off down the hall. "We're going to have a talk with Mr. Kingsley."

"Uh, whatever you say, Mr. Applegate," said Joe. He looked back at the receptionist. She was staring at them, her mouth open.

Hurd strode up to a pair of wooden doors with the name *Barrett Kingsley III* emblazoned across them in gold letters and threw them wide open. Inside was an office that looked as though it stretched halfway to the end of the block, with carpeting so thick it seemed to need mowing. Seated at a large marble desk at the far end of the room was a middle-aged man with thinning black hair. He was wearing a dignified gray suit and dark-rimmed glasses.

"Mr. Kingsley," announced Hurd, striding into the room as if he owned the place, "I've come to make you a proposition. Your grandfather bought an island from my father many years ago, and I'd like to buy it back—for sentimental reasons, of course. Its name is Granite Cay."

Kingsley leaned forward, as though he were about to speak. But he was cut off by a voice from the far corner of the room.

"You're too late, Applegate," the voice said.

"What?" said Hurd, stopping so suddenly that Chet nearly collided with him from behind. "What was that? Who said that?"

"I said you're too late, Applegate," the voice continued. *"I've* just bought Granite Cay!"

3 Three-Way Split

Looking across the room, Frank and Joe saw the man who had just spoken. He had white hair and was massively built. He wore a gray suit nearly identical to Barrett Kingsley's and had a ruddy complexion and piercing black eyes that stared intently at Hurd Applegate. As soon as he had finished making his announcement about Granite Cay, the man leaned back in his chair, a smug grin on his face.

"Vernon Prescott!" exclaimed Hurd. "What are you doing here?"

"Same thing you are, Applegate," Prescott replied, a thick Texas twang in his voice. "Looking to buy a little real estate."

Joe turned to Frank. "Vernon Prescott?" he whispered. "Isn't he . . . ?"

21

". . . the developer who bought the Tower Mansion," Frank whispered back. "Right."

"What's your interest in Granite Cay?" Hurd demanded angrily.

"I've been interested in Granite Cay for years," Prescott replied matter-of-factly. "It's a choice piece of land."

"What a coincidence," muttered Frank.

"Hah!" cried Hurd. "It was those three workmen you sent to my mansion, wasn't it? They must have called you, to tell you about the . . . the . . ."

Prescott raised his eyebrows. "Yes, Hurd?" he asked innocently. "Tell me about what?"

"I'd like to know what everybody's talking about," bellowed Barrett Kingsley III from behind his huge desk.

"It's nothing," said Hurd, an unconvincing look of wide-eyed innocence on his face. "I want to buy back some land that once belonged to my father, that's all."

"I don't believe either one of you," announced Kingsley. "There's something very suspicious going on here."

"I think you'd better tell the whole story, Mr. Applegate," said Frank.

"Right," said Joe. "Mr. Kingsley's going to find out sooner or later, so you might as well just tell him."

"Who are these young men?" Kingsley asked. "I don't believe we've been properly introduced."

"I'm Frank Hardy," said Frank, nodding politely at the older man.

"I'm Joe Hardy," added his brother. "And this is our friend Chet Morton."

"Are you, ah, business associates of Mr. Applegate?" asked Kingsley, frowning.

"Not exactly," said Joe. "We're detectives. You might have heard of our father, Fenton Hardy. He's a detective, too."

"Detectives?" asked Kingsley. "Oh, yes, I've met your father. And I think I've heard of you, too. So what's this about having something to tell me?"

"I think Mr. Applegate had better tell the story," said Joe.

Hurd glanced at the Hardys for a moment. Then he sighed deeply. "Oh, very well," he said. "Maybe you're right. I have in my possession a map that shows the location of buried treasure on Granite Cay."

"Buried treasure?" said Kingsley, unsuccessfully hiding a smile. "You've got to be kidding."

"No. My father was searching for a treasure and believed that he had found it on Granite Cay," said Hurd.

"But he never dug it up?" Kingsley asked.

"I'm positive he didn't. He sold the island to your grandfather to pay off his debts."

"And you think you can find this treasure on Granite Cay?" asked Kingsley, apparently beginning to take Hurd's story seriously.

"Yes, I do," Hurd said confidently.

"If there's going to be a treasure hunt," announced Prescott loudly, "it's going to be conducted by Prescott Enterprises. Do I have to remind you all that I just bought Granite Cay?"

"Um, technically that's not true," said Kingsley. "We've discussed the arrangements and worked out the details, but there's no signed bill of sale. And until there *is* a bill of sale, the island is still mine."

Prescott looked flustered. "But—but—"

"It looks like you've been withholding a few important facts from me, Vernon."

"What?" Prescott sputtered. "I don't know what you're talking about! I had no idea that there was treasure on Granite Cay!"

"I suppose the workmen didn't listen in on our conversation and tell you about the treasure map?" said Frank.

"What's this about a map?" asked Kingsley. "Do you have this map with you, Hurd?"

"Of course not," Hurd replied indignantly. "The map is in my private possession, where it will remain."

"I see," said Kingsley. "Perhaps I can offer to buy that map from you, Hurd."

Hurd's face turned a deep red. "Absolutely not!

The map was my father's, and I have no intention of parting with it."

"Perhaps I *have* heard a few things about this treasure map," added Prescott cautiously.

"So you admit it!" Hurd cried triumphantly. "You admit that you've been spying on me!"

"I've got an idea," interrupted Frank. "If nobody minds my making a suggestion, that is."

"Go ahead, young man," said Kingsley.

"Well," said Frank, "I was thinking that you and Mr. Applegate and Mr. Prescott might go into a—what do you call it—a joint venture?"

"That's the term, all right," said Kingsley. "You mean we should team up, pool our resources?"

"Exactly," said Frank. "It looks like both Mr. Applegate and Mr. Prescott know where the treasure is, but you're the one who owns the island. Maybe you could work out some kind of three-way deal. Each of you could pitch in money and manpower. And if there turns out to be a treasure, you could split it three ways."

Kingsley nodded. "Not a bad idea," he said. "I'd certainly be willing to discuss the possibility. Assuming that Mr. Applegate and Mr. Prescott are also willing."

Hurd Applegate and Vernon Prescott looked at each other and then nodded grudgingly.

"Fine, then. It's settled," said Kingsley. He thought for a moment. Then he said, "Here's the deal I'm prepared to offer: Applegate supplies the map, I supply the island, and Prescott Enterprises supplies the digging equipment, not to mention Vernon Prescott's continued silence on the subject of buried treasure. Agreed?"

"If there does turn out to be a treasure," said Hurd, "how will the proceeds be divided among us?"

"An even three-way split," said Kingsley. "Each of us gets a third. But someone has to decide how the treasure will be disposed of. If it's in the form of old gold coins we might want to auction them to collectors, then keep the money for ourselves. If it's an artifact of some kind—say, an old statue or some relic—we can sell it to a museum or to someone who collects that kind of thing."

"And you should bring in an outside expert. Somebody who knows about buried treasure and can make a decision about what to do with it," added Frank.

"That's a good suggestion," Kingsley said.

"Right," said Joe. "And maybe this outside expert should know *how* to dig up buried treasure."

"Do you have someone in mind?" asked Kingsley.

"Um," mumbled Joe, "I don't really know anybody . . ."

"I do," said Frank, snapping his fingers. "There was an article in the Sunday paper a couple of weeks ago about this archaeologist who lives a few miles out of town. He teaches at a local college part-time, and he's led several important archaeological expeditions. The article said that he'd just helped bring up a pirate galleon in the Bahamas. I bet he knows a lot about buried treasure."

"What was his name?" asked Kingsley.

Frank thought for a moment. "Rupert Damien, I think. Yes, Professor Rupert Damien."

"I remember that article," said Joe. "He was in some kind of legal dispute over the rights to the pirate ship he'd raised. He wanted the contents to go to a museum."

"I think I've heard of him," said Kingsley. "He's supposed to be pretty good. I guess we couldn't ask for a better supervisor for our treasure hunt. After all, archaeologists specialize in digging up buried artifacts. Of course, Mr. Applegate and Mr. Prescott have yet to agree to our expedition."

"Well," said Hurd hesitantly, "I suppose it sounds fair."

"What about you, Prescott?" asked Kingsley.

"Oh, all right," Prescott growled. "I guess I don't have any choice. It's a deal, though I won't pretend I like it."

The three men stood and shook hands with one another across the table.

Kingsley turned to the others. "I'll have the

papers drawn up. They'll be ready for your signatures tomorrow morning. I'll contact Rupert Damien and see if he'll agree to go along."

"So when do we start digging?" asked Prescott.

"How about tomorrow?" suggested Kingsley. "As soon as the contracts are signed."

"These guys work fast," Chet said under his breath to the Hardys.

"Tomorrow?" said Prescott.

"That shouldn't be any problem for Prescott Enterprises," said Kingsley. "You've got the men in your employ already, and I know you have the equipment. I'll supply a small boat; you just bring your team of treasure hunters down to Kingsley Marina in the morning and sign the papers. I'll worry about the other details."

"Now, just a minute," said Hurd. "I don't like having the two of you running this operation by yourselves. I want some of my own people on this team."

"Okay," said Kingsley. "Who did you have in mind?"

"Well," said Hurd, gesturing toward Joe, Frank, and Chet. "How about these young men here?"

Chet's mouth fell open. "Us?" he said. "Dig up treasure?"

"I have no objection," said Kingsley. "What about you, Vernon?"

Prescott shrugged. "It's okay with me."

"Well," said Joe, "it does sound pretty exciting. Okay, I'll go along."

"Me, too," said Frank.

"Count me in," added Chet.

"Then it's settled," said Barrett Kingsley, rising to his feet. "I'll see all of you at the marina tomorrow morning, bright and early. I almost wish I were going along myself. But I'm afraid I have too much work to do here."

The group split up moments later. The Hardys and Chet left the building and piled into the Hardys' van along with Hurd Applegate. When they arrived back at Tower Mansion, Hurd sat in thought for a moment before leaving the van.

"I'm worried about the map," he said. "I want you to take care of it tonight, so that nothing happens to it."

"Don't worry about the map, Mr. Applegate," said Frank. "We have a safe at home. We can put it there."

They left the van and headed back up the hill to the mansion. When she saw them arrive, Adelia Applegate hurried Chet off to the kitchen for some tea and chocolate cake. Hurd led the Hardys back up to his apartment in the old tower. The map was still on the desk in the secret room.

Joe tucked the map into a dusty manila folder and placed the folder under his arm. As they started back down, he and Frank paused for a moment at

29

the top of the stairs while Hurd hurried back to the main part of the house.

"This place really does bring back memories," Joe said.

"Yeah," said Frank. "Isn't this the spot where you fell off the stairs and nearly broke your neck?"

Joe turned red. "That was an accident. It could have happened to anyone. Besides, I caught myself on the landing before I could get hurt."

"Yeah, right," said Frank with a laugh. "Only a real klutz would have fallen off in the first place. At least the Applegates repaired the railing here so that nobody else will fall off."

Frank reached out and tested the banister, rattling it gently with his hands. Then he leaned on it to test its strength.

"See?" said Frank. "I can't even fall off the edge when I try. I guess I just don't have your gift for—"

Suddenly the railing snapped, the wood giving way like a fragile toothpick. Frank flailed his arms wildly in the air, frantically struggling to keep his balance.

He failed. All at once he was falling into a stairwell four stories deep!

4 The Hunt Begins

Frank felt his brother's hand reach out and grab one of his legs. For a second it seemed as if Frank's weight was going to pull Joe into the stairwell, too. Then Joe dug in his heels and tugged at Frank's leg with all his strength, pulling him back onto the landing.

Frank collapsed to the floor, his face pale. "Thanks," he said breathlessly.

"So who were you calling a klutz?" Joe demanded.

"Klutz?" Frank said innocently. "I don't remember saying anything about a klutz."

"Right," said Joe, rolling his eyes. "Must be temporary amnesia after your accident. Well, I happen to remember that Hurd, Adelia, and Chet

31

are waiting downstairs with tea and chocolate cake, and it looks to me like you could use some of both."

"What are we waiting for?" Frank asked. "Let's get down there before Chet scarfs up the whole cake."

"Rise and shine!" shouted Joe Hardy the next morning at seven. "Time to go treasure hunting!"

"Uh-huh," muttered Frank, as he crawled out of bed. "You're really excited about this, aren't you?"

"You bet," said Joe.

"We don't even know that there's any treasure at all," said Frank, heading for the bathroom.

"There's definitely treasure," said Joe. "I can feel it in my bones. Just wait and see."

Two hours later, the Hardys and Chet Morton pulled into the driveway of Kingsley Marina. The marina was located on Barmet Bay, about three miles from Tower Mansion. Frank parked the van in the middle of the gravel parking lot. Then he and Joe and Chet got out of the van and headed for the dock, pulling on khaki-colored knapsacks full of food and supplies.

Hurd Applegate, Vernon Prescott, and Barrett Kingsley stood on the dock in front of a dozen or so private boats.

"Right on time," said Barrett Kingsley. "The whole team's here, except for Professor Damien, who should arrive at any minute."

Standing next to Prescott were three familiar-looking figures.

"Uh-oh," Frank said softly to Joe and Chet. "It's the three workmen from the mansion."

"There's something about those guys I don't like," said Joe.

"Did you bring the map?" Hurd asked, stepping up to the Hardys and pulling them aside.

"We made a photocopy and put the original in our safe," Frank said.

Joe pointed to his knapsack. "The copy's right here, Mr. Applegate."

"Good," Hurd said approvingly.

Vernon Prescott looked sourly at the Hardys. "Well, I guess I'd better introduce you folks." He beckoned to the three workmen. "Jack, Bill, George—I want you to meet Frank and Joe Hardy and their friend Chet Morton."

"Yeah," said the burly man with the cigar in his mouth. "I think we've met already. My name's George Lewin." He gave the three boys a grudging smile and shook their hands briskly.

"Jack Kruger," muttered the second man, without smiling. He looked as if he spent most of his time lifting weights. His denim jacket had been cut off at the shoulders and his shirt sleeves were rolled up to reveal thick, tattooed biceps.

"Not a very talkative fellow," whispered Joe.

33

"When you're built like that," Frank said, "you don't *need* to talk much."

The third man had two menacing, half-closed eyes and at least two days' growth of beard on his face. He studied the three teens carefully before shaking hands. "I'm Bill Drake. You kids just do what the grown-ups tell you on this little treasure hunt and we'll get along real well." He smiled and rejoined his companions.

"Kids? Grown-ups?" Joe said, his face turning red. "What's that supposed to mean?"

"Take it easy, Joe," Frank said quietly. "We have to get along with those guys."

"Ah," said Kingsley. "It looks like Professor Damien's arrived."

A dark green jeep, its tires spattered with mud, rattled into the parking lot. An older man in a battered hunting jacket climbed out and walked toward the crowd.

"Good to see you, Professor Damien," said Kingsley, when the man reached them. "I'm glad you could join us."

Rupert Damien was a short, wiry man who looked to be about sixty years old. He had coppery red hair and a ragged beard, and he wore dark green shorts that revealed muscular, well-tanned legs. Slung over one shoulder was a battered khaki knapsack bulging with odd shapes. The tools of the archaeologist's trade, Frank guessed, admiring the professor's confident stride. He thought Damien looked like a man who had come face-to-face with danger in every part of the world—and loved every minute of it.

Damien held out his hand to Barrett Kingsley and smiled.

"You must be Mr. Kingsley," he said. "Glad to be here. Wouldn't miss this expedition for the world."

Kingsley introduced Damien to the others.

"Well," Damien said briskly, "if the boat's ready, why don't we get started?"

"Right this way," said Kingsley, leading the group down the dock. At one end, a large cabin cruiser was waiting, with a large pile of equipment on the deck, including shovels, picks, trowels, several ropes, a large bucket, a hand-operated drill, a transistor radio, and a lantern.

"Excellent," said Damien. "We used a boat much like this in the Bahamas."

He grabbed the rungs of a wooden ladder attached to the dock and lowered himself onto the deck of the boat. The Hardys and Chet followed, then George, Bill, and Jack.

"If you need anything else," said Prescott, "just radio back to shore, and I'll have it waiting for you when you get back from the island."

Damien examined a boxy gadget fastened next to

the helm. "The radio appears to be in working order," he said. "Everything's shipshape. Let's cast off."

"Good luck," said Kingsley. "Radio a report back to us if you find treasure."

Hurd nodded to the Hardys, as Bill untied the rope that moored them to the dock. Jack grabbed a pole and pushed the boat away from the mooring posts, then Damien fired up the engine and they sputtered into Barmet Bay.

The day was good for boating. It had been cloudy earlier, but patches of blue sky had already broken through. The water was calm, but there was a cool, stiff breeze. Joe buttoned his windbreaker and grabbed the rail that ran around the deck, staring out at the bay.

"This is great!" he said. "A boat trip and a chance to dig up buried treasure."

Professor Damien had turned on the radio to a staticky shortwave weather station. The announcer was talking about Hurricane Celia, which was threatening the North Carolina coast.

"I'm glad that storm's a long way off," said Joe.

"I wouldn't worry," said Frank. "Hurricanes almost never get this far north."

"I just wish those guys would stop staring at us," Chet said. He jerked his head at George, Bill, and Jack, who were leaning on the railing on the opposite side of the deck. Bill whispered something in George's ear and George laughed. The muscular Jack Kruger stood quietly with his massive arms folded across his chest.

"Don't worry about those guys," said Frank. "They're probably harmless. Don't bother them, and they won't bother us."

"I hope you're right," said Chet.

"I love the sea," announced Damien at the helm, speaking to no one in particular. "Did you know that Barmet Bay was discovered in 1574 by the Dutch explorer Henrik Shuusten? He said that its waters were 'as beautiful as those of the unchanging Nile.' Of course, Shuusten had never seen the Nile."

"Uh, no," said Frank, turning from the railing. "I didn't know that. Did you know that, Joe?"

"I can't say I did," Joe said.

"I knew that," said Chet. "He called it Baarmuter Bay. It was named after some important person in Holland."

Joe looked at Chet through narrowed eyes. "When did you become such a walking encyclopedia?" he asked.

"I learned it in history. That was a great class."

"I thought you were an archaeologist," said Frank to Damien. "Not a historian."

Damien looked up with a smile. "An archaeologist is a little of both, I guess. Archaeology is a kind of tangible history. We dig up the past so that we can touch it, make it a little more real."

"So what do you think about this treasure story?" asked Joe. "Do you think there could be treasure on Granite Cay?"

"Yes, I do," said Damien. "It's little known to the general public, but this area of the Atlantic Coast was frequented by pirates in the seventeenth century."

"Did they leave a lot of treasure behind?" asked Chet.

"Not really," said Damien. "They had much better things to do with their booty than to leave it in holes in the ground. Still, buried treasure does exist around here."

"So when are we going to reach Granite Cay?" Frank asked, turning back toward the marina. The dock from which they had departed already looked very small and far away.

"About half an hour, I'd say," Damien told him. "It's at the mouth of the Atlantic Ocean, where Shuusten himself sailed into the bay. It was a perfect docking site for pirates."

For the rest of the trip to Granite Cay, the Hardys and Chet remained at the front of the ship, talking with Damien about archaeology and the discovery of Barmet Bay, while George, Bill, and Jack remained aft. Occasionally, the Hardys heard them roar with laughter.

Finally Damien raised his arm above the helm and pointed to a sharp spit of rock that seemed to rise out of the waves.

"There she is," Damien announced. "Granite Cay."

"A rock?" asked Joe. "We're looking for treasure on a rock?"

As they drew closer, however, it became obvious that the rock was actually a sharp stone cliff thrusting upward at one end of what was otherwise a low, tree-covered island. Just below the cliff, two arms of land extended into the bay, forming a natural harbor. Damien steered the boat toward it.

Frank looked up at the rock and said, "Now I see how the island got its name. I wonder if that's really granite?"

Damien brought the cabin cruiser as close to the beach as he could without running it aground. "Someone drop the anchor," he ordered, pointing to a large piece of metal tethered to the deck on a long, coiled rope.

Frank grabbed the anchor and tried to lift it. To his surprise, the weight of the anchor practically pulled him down onto the deck.

"Wow, that's heavy," he gasped, backing away.

"That's the idea," said Joe. "It's supposed to hold the ship in place."

Without glancing at Frank, Jack Kruger picked up the anchor and tossed it over the side as easily as though he were dunking a basketball.

Frank edged closer to Joe. "Promise me you won't get in a fight with that guy," he whispered.

"Huh? Why?"

"Because his muscles have muscles, you dipstick. He probably uses guys like us for barbells."

"Come on," said Damien. "We're going to wade ashore."

One by one, the shipmates took off their shoes, rolled up their pants, and climbed over the side into the water. The water was cold but only came to knee level. Everybody grabbed a handful of equipment and lugged it to the beach.

The beach was narrow and covered with a rough bed of pebbles, driftwood, and flotsam that had floated in on the tide. The professor was the last to come ashore.

"What now?" asked Frank.

"I was told that you were bringing a map," said Damien. "It would be a good idea to consult it."

"Okay," said Joe, pulling the plastic-covered photocopy out of his knapsack. "But be careful with it. If you lose that copy, we'll have to go back to Bayport for another."

"Don't worry," said Damien. "I'll treat it with respect." He took it from Joe and examined both sides carefully.

40

"The markings are rather inexact," he said finally. "But I'm pretty sure the treasure is in the southeast corner of the island, through those woods." He pointed to some trees on a rise above the beach.

"So let's head southeast," said Joe. "Grab your equipment, everybody."

"Do you mind if I hold on to this map?" Damien asked Joe. "It should come in handy."

"Go ahead," said Joe. "Hurd won't mind."

Shovels and machinery in hand, the group began marching into the woods. The trees were sparse, and the ground was covered with only a thin layer of vegetation, making the trip an easy one.

"Which way is southeast, anyway?" asked Chet.

"That way," said Damien, gesturing deeper into the woods. "According to the map, there should be a clearing ahead, though it's hard to say precisely where it is. We'll just have to circle this general area until we stumble across it."

"Maybe we should split up and walk about thirty feet apart," said Frank. "That way we'll be more likely to find it. The first one to see the clearing calls out to the others."

"Big-shot teenager, giving orders," muttered Bill Drake.

Frank glanced over at him. He wondered if Bill was going to start trouble, but the sullen-faced man said nothing else.

"Sounds good to me," said Joe.

"Very well," said Damien. "Everyone fan out. Frank, Joe, and Chet, you go that way; you men follow the outer rim of the woods."

The group did as Damien asked. Joe found himself walking through a stand of oak trees. Just to his right, he saw a large open area.

Could that be the clearing Damien was talking about? he wondered. Not likely. On the map the treasure had looked to be within viewing distance of the beach, but this clearing was still deep inside the woods. He struck out toward it, anyway.

The cleared area was about twenty feet wide and covered with glistening mud. No, Joe decided, this wasn't what they were looking for. He shrugged and started across, hurrying toward the trees on the opposite side.

Suddenly the ground seemed to drop out from under him. He pitched forward and the shovels he was carrying flew out of his grasp and across the clearing. He struck the ground on his hands and knees and seemed to sink right into the earth itself. His legs disappeared into the mud, and he could hear a slurping sound.

This wasn't mud, he realized suddenly. It was quicksand. And he was sinking right into the middle of it!

5 The Treasure Pit

"He-e-e-e-e-elp!" Joe shouted at the top of his lungs. "Get me out of here!"

He felt the quicksand sucking him into the ground, pulling on him like a giant hand. Quickly he shrugged off his knapsack and tossed it to dry ground. Then he twisted and turned to try to free himself, but his struggling only seemed to make him sink deeper.

Where were the others? he wondered. Had they heard him?

The quicksand was up to his waist now and rising quickly. The entire lower portion of his body felt as though it were encased in hardening cement.

"He-e-e-e-elp!" he shouted again.

Frank came dashing out of the woods to his right. Seconds later, Chet appeared from the left.

"What's the matter?" Frank shouted.

"What's all the racket?" Chet called.

"Quicksand!" Joe gasped. "I can't get out."

"Here," said Frank, rushing toward him. "I'll give you a hand."

"No," said Joe. "Don't get too close. You'll sink in it, too!"

"Okay, okay," said Frank. "Just don't panic. That's the worst thing you can do."

"I'm *trying* not to," said Joe, the quicksand rising nearly to his chest, "but I'm panicking, anyway. The harder I try to get out of here, the harder it sucks me in."

"Then stop trying to get out," Chet said.

"Chet's right," Frank said. "Thrashing around like that makes you sink. Just relax and lie on your back, like you're floating in water."

"All right," said Joe, trying to calm his nerves. "I'm relaxing. Kind of."

Suddenly Professor Damien appeared out of the woods, huffing and puffing. George, Bill, and Jack were just behind him.

"I heard the shouting," Damien said. "What's going on?"

"Stay back, Professor," Frank warned. "Joe's caught in quicksand."

"I don't think I'm sinking anymore," Joe said. "Now what do I do?"

44

"Swim," said Damien.

"Swim?" asked Joe.

"Yes," answered Damien. "Swim toward me with a backstroke. Surely you know how."

"Well, yes," said Joe. "I've just never done it in quicksand before."

He began to backstroke toward Damien, almost as though he were actually in a pool. The quicksand was shallower around the edges of the clearing and after he had swum a couple of yards, Chet and Frank grabbed him and helped lift him up. The quicksand made sucking noises as they pulled him out of it. Gobs of wet sand fell off Joe's jacket and pants.

"If you're all right, Joe," said Damien, not wasting any time, "I suggest that we continue looking for the clearing."

"I think I saw a beach over this way," said Frank, pointing to the south. "Do you think that might be what we're looking for?"

"Could be," said Damien. "Let's continue in that direction, then. We'd all better stay together, after what happened to Joe."

"I'll go along with that," said Joe.

Joe retrieved his knapsack and the shovels he'd been carrying and started off again with the group. A few minutes later, the woods came to an end, and they found themselves standing in a wide grass- and mud-covered clearing above another pebble-covered beach.

"This looks like it might be the spot," said Damien.

"So where's the treasure?" Chet asked.

"Yeah," said Joe. "If we just start digging in any old place it might take years to find the treasure."

"Patience," said Damien.

The archaeologist looked around for a moment. Then he walked to one of the trees that bordered the clearing, gripped the tree with both hands, and shimmied up into its branches.

"Much better," he shouted, surveying the area from about ten feet above the ground. "I'm getting a wonderful view from up here. Ah, yes. I think I see something there." He pointed toward the eastern edge of the clearing.

"What do you see?" asked Joe. "An old skull and crossbones marking the site?"

"There's a spot where the ground is slightly sunken," said Damien. "Roughly circular, with sparser vegetation than the surrounding area. Someone might have dug there a very long time ago, which would account for the vegetation growing back differently."

"I don't see anything," said Frank.

"Me, neither," said Joe.

"It takes a trained eye—and the right vantage

46

point," said Damien, climbing back down the tree. He dropped to the ground and headed toward the spot he had just been pointing to.

"Unless I miss my guess, this is where our treasure is," Damien announced.

Bill Drake grunted. "Grab your shovels, you guys. Here's where we earn our pay."

"How deep do you think the treasure is buried?" asked Joe.

"There's no way to tell," said Damien. "We can only dig and find out."

"Are you going to dig with us, Professor?" asked Frank.

"I'm afraid I'm getting a little old for that," Damien said. "The doctors tell me I have to start watching out for my heart. But I'll be helping out in whatever way possible."

Chet took the transistor radio, which he had carried from the boat, and tuned it to a rock station, so that they could listen while they worked.

Jack Kruger took a large pickax and began breaking up the hardened soil. The others took shovels and began digging at various places, piling the dirt to one side of the depression.

Almost immediately, Chet's shovel struck something hard. He crouched and pulled a flat, squarish piece of rock out of the ground.

"Flagstone," said Damien. "That wouldn't occur

naturally in a spot like this. My guess is that someone left it to mark the location of the treasure."

"Great!" said Joe. "That means the treasure really does exist."

"Not necessarily," said Damien. "But it's a good sign."

Over the next few minutes, several more flagstones were uncovered. Bill Drake pulled up a flagstone, scowled at it, and handed it to Professor Damien.

"This one's pretty messed up, Professor," he said. "Looks like somebody's been writing on it."

Damien took a brush from his backpack and carefully removed the dirt clinging to the stone. Then he turned it over in his hands while examining it with a magnifying lens. "Yes," he said finally. "The writing looks like some sort of code."

Frank peered over Damien's shoulder. "It looks like a cryptogram, the kind they have in the Sunday paper. May I take a look at it?"

"Be my guest," Damien said, handing the stone to Frank.

On one side of the flat stone were some carved letters:

GLXHGM ZXXG QXOWL OVXU GJX
TDXFGXUG GDXFUYDX WZ GJXB FOO.

"It's total gibberish," said Joe.

"No," said Frank. "I'm pretty sure it's a substitution code. Each letter stands for a different letter of the alphabet. All we have to do is put the correct letters in place of the substitutes."

"That's all?" said Joe doubtfully. "But how do you know which letter stands for what?"

"First you count the letters," said Frank.

George turned to the other workmen and twirled his finger at his temple. "The kid's crazy," he said. "He thinks he can read that rock."

"Look," said Frank, pointing to the writing on the stone. "The most common letter in this message is X. There are eleven of them. The most common letter in the English language is E, so X probably stands for E. Anybody got a piece of paper?"

Damien pulled a notebook from his pack and ripped a page out of it. "Here," he said. "Use this."

Frank took the paper and pulled a pencil out of his pocket. On a clean sheet of paper he carefully wrote down the letters from the flagstone.

"Now I'll just write E's over all the X's," said Frank. He wrote the following on the paper:

```
  E       EE     E          E      E
 E   E       E       E          E
GLXHGM  ZXXG  QXOWL  OVXU  GJX
TDXFGXUG  GDXFUYDX  WZ  GJXB  FOO
```

49

"That makes a lot of sense," said Joe sarcastically. "What are you going to do now?"

"Well," said Frank, "this word that looks like GJX is probably *THE*, which means that *G* stands for *T* and *J* stands for *H*." He carefully wrote the new letters onto the paper:

```
T  E  T     EET   E          E    THE
TDE  TE  T T  E THE  E
T E T EET E E THE E TE T T E E GLXHGM
ZXXG  QXOWL  OVXU  GJX  TDXFGXUG
GDXFUYDX WZ GJXB FOO
```

"It's as clear as mud," said Joe, looking at the results.

"Don't get so frustrated and discouraged," said Frank. "I think I see a couple more words here. Uh-huh. . . ."

Frank spent a few more minutes scribbling letters, studying the results, erasing, then scribbling more letters. As he worked the others stared at him, their shovels lying forgotten by their sides. Finally, Frank's eyes lit up.

"I've got it!" he said excitedly. "It's a message, all right!"

"What does it say?" asked Chet.

"By all means, share it with the rest of us," said Damien.

Triumphantly, Frank handed over the sheet of paper to Professor Damien. The deciphered message read:

TWENTY FEET BELOW LIES THE GREATEST TREASURE OF THEM ALL

6 Doorway to Nowhere

"This is great!" shouted Chet. "Buried treasure! I can't wait to see what it is!"

George chomped on his cigar and stared at Frank with newfound respect. "I've got to give you credit, kid," he said. "I didn't think you would really figure out what it said on that rock. Maybe you're not just a dumb teenager after all."

"Thanks," said Frank, surprised at the compliment. "I think."

"Well, let's dig," George said, turning away and grabbing his shovel. "Or are you kids just gonna stand around jawing?"

"I'm ready," said Frank. "Come on, everybody. Let's get back to work."

The digging continued. There were no more

flagstones and no more messages. As the pit grew deeper, the diggers had to toss the dirt higher and higher to clear the sides of the pit—and the work grew more and more difficult. Finally, Professor Damien signaled everyone to stop.

"Lunch break?" Chet asked hopefully.

"If you like, yes," said Damien. "But we also need a better way to remove debris. Did someone bring the ropes from the boat?"

"I did," said Jack Kruger. "There are five. I left them over on the edge of the woods."

"Bring two of them here and give me a hand," said Damien.

"I vote that the rest of us have lunch," said Chet.

"I'll second that," said Joe.

"Not a bad idea," said George.

As the others climbed out of the pit and began opening their lunch bags, Jack Kruger walked to the woods and picked up two thick coils of rope. He carried them back to Damien, who pointed to a stout tree limb overhanging the pit.

"Throw one rope over the limb," Damien said. "We can use the limb as a pulley to bring up buckets of dirt."

"I was wondering what the bucket was for," Chet said.

"Well, now you know," said Damien. "Would you get the bucket for me, Chet?"

"Me and my big mouth," said Chet, putting his lunch aside.

Damien tied one end of the rope, which was now draped over the tree limb, to the thick handle of the metal bucket. Then he tied the other end of the rope to a sturdy tree root that protruded from the ground not far from the pit.

"There," he said. "A little makeshift, but that should make an effective pulley. I'd like those of you working in the pit to empty your shovels into the bucket. Then Jack will haul up the bucket when it's full. I'll put a few knots in the second rope and lower it into the pit, so that you can use it to climb out when the hole gets too deep."

When lunch ended, the group climbed back into the pit and the work resumed. By early afternoon, the pit was roughly five feet deep and the crew of diggers could barely see over the edge. Jack Kruger repeatedly hauled buckets full of dirt out of the hole and dumped them in a growing pile in the middle of the clearing.

"My back is going to ache for a week," Chet moaned, as he dumped another shovelful of dirt into the bucket.

"It's good exercise," said Frank. "Think how strong your back will be when football practice starts."

"My back'll be *broken* when football practice starts," Chet moaned.

"You kids are wimps," Bill Drake said with a laugh. "Why don't you step aside and let us men do the work?"

"Forget it," said Joe, tightening his grip on his shovel. "We 'kids' are as tough as you are. Right, guys?" he added, looking at Frank and Chet.

"Yeah, sure," Chet mumbled, rolling his eyes.

The digging continued. As bucket after bucket was filled with dirt, the pit grew deeper and deeper. By the time they reached the ten-foot mark, the only part of the outside world still visible to the diggers was the blue sky above the pit and the tree limb from which the bucket was hanging.

Suddenly Frank's shovel struck something hard, making a loud metallic scraping sound.

"What was that?" asked Chet.

"I don't know," said Frank. "But I think I've found something."

"The treasure?" asked Joe.

"It can't be the treasure," said George, the ever-present cigar still tucked in his mouth. "That rock you found said the treasure was twenty feet deep, and we haven't gone more than ten."

"Maybe the rock was wrong," said Joe.

"Just help me uncover whatever it is I found," said Frank, kneeling in the dirt. He brushed aside gobs of dirt to reveal a rusty metal surface.

"That's definitely man-made," Joe said. "Hey, Professor! I think we found something."

Damien's tanned face appeared above the rim. "Wonderful," he said, smiling. "What does it look like?"

"Some kind of metal," Frank said. "Rusty. It made a kind of hollow sound when I hit it with my shovel."

"Be careful with it," said Damien. "Don't damage it. It may be a valuable artifact."

After a few minutes they had uncovered the entire metal surface. It was about four feet square. At one end was a crude metal handle.

"It looks like some kind of lid," said Frank. "This handle must open it."

"The lid of the treasure chest!" Chet crowed. "All right!"

"Pull on the handle gently," said Damien from above. "See if it will open."

Frank yanked on the handle, softly at first and then with more force. The lid didn't budge.

"Let me do that," snapped Bill Drake. "You kids are cream puffs."

"Go easy on them, Bill," said George. "We may be down here together for a long time."

"Not if I can help it," said Bill. He grasped the handle with both hands and tugged at it with all his strength. The muscles in his neck bulged, and his face turned red.

"Don't strain yourself, Bill," said Joe. "We really don't want to have to carry you back to the boat."

"Put a cork in it, kid," Bill sneered. "I've . . . almost . . . got it."

Suddenly he roared with pain and dropped the handle. "My back!" he screamed. "I've thrown my back out!"

"Terrific," said Chet. "One less guy to do the digging."

"Well," said Frank, "if Hercules there can't open the lid, I'm sure not going to try."

"Let's get Jack Kruger down here," Joe suggested. "He has major muscles. He might be able to do it."

"I have a better idea," said Damien. "I'll remove the bucket from the rope and toss the rope down to you, then you can tie it around the handle. If all of us pull on the rope at once, we might be able to open the lid."

The professor disappeared from view for a moment, then reappeared, tossing the rope down to the diggers. Frank lashed it around the handle, securing it with his best knot. Then the group climbed up the other rope, with Bill Drake complaining loudly about his injured back.

"All right, everybody," Professor Damien said. "Grab the rope. When I count to three, pull as hard as you can."

The group did as he asked, the muscular Jack Kruger taking the end of the rope and Damien himself taking the position closest to the pit. Even

57

Bill Drake, whose back pain seemed to be subsiding, joined in.

"Just like a tug of war," said Chet.

"I hope we win," added Joe.

"Everybody ready?" asked Damien. "One. Two. Three!"

With a loud chorus of grunts, the pulling began. At first they couldn't budge the lid, and for a second Frank thought they'd burn off the skin of their palms before the lid popped open. Then, all at once, the rope moved, causing everyone to tumble to the ground.

"I think we did it," Chet said.

"Treasure, here we come!" cried Joe.

Jack Kruger lashed the rope back over the tree limb to keep the lid from snapping shut again. Frank, Joe, and Chet lowered themselves back into the pit, followed by Bill and George.

Sure enough, the metal lid was now ajar. Frank untied the rope and opened the lid the rest of the way. It groaned rustily, then fell open against one side of the pit.

"What's inside?" said Joe. "Gold and jewels?"

"Let's take a look," said Frank, kneeling beside the opening.

He peered through the hole, letting his eyes adjust to the darkness. Gradually the interior of the hole became visible. It was not a treasure chest. The narrow hole widened into an earthen chamber about as wide as the pit they were digging and several feet deep.

"What do you know?" said Frank. "This wasn't the lid of a chest. It was a door."

"A door to what?" Joe asked.

"Some kind of room," Frank said.

"Who wants to go inside first?" Frank asked.

"I'll go," Bill volunteered.

"You'll need a lantern," Professor Damien called down. "I'll lower one to you on the rope."

He tied the battery-operated lantern to the rope and lowered it into Bill's hands. Bill switched it on and swung his legs into the hole.

When his feet touched bottom, he stood up straight. His head was almost level with the top of the hole. "It's about six feet deep," he called up. After a few moments he added, "There isn't much in here that I can see. Just dirt."

"And we could sure use more of that," Chet commented dryly.

"I'll help you look around," said Joe, lowering himself into the chamber after Bill. "You might miss something important."

"Wait a minute," said Bill, from inside the chamber. "There's some kind of hole in one of the walls."

"Where?" asked Joe. He crouched next to Bill and studied the wall as the man held the lantern next to it. Clearly visible in the dim glow was a square hole set right into the middle of the wall. It was about twelve inches across and had surprisingly smooth edges.

"What is it?" asked Frank, peering into the chamber.

"It looks like some kind of tunnel," said Joe, "but it's too small to get into."

"Then what's it for?" asked Frank.

"This may sound crazy," said Joe, "but I think I hear gurgling water inside it."

"Yeah," said Bill. "I hear it, too."

"Gurgling water?" asked Frank. "Maybe you've discovered some pirate plumbing. A drinking fountain for thirsty treasure buriers."

"How about thirsty treasure hunters?" said Chet. "I'd like a drink about now. My canteen's empty."

"It's getting louder," said Joe, putting his ear to the hole. "It's—it's almost like the water's coming toward us!"

Suddenly a spray of water hit his head and trickled down his neck.

"Let's get out of here!" said Bill, a sudden panic in his voice. "Something funny's going on!"

"It's only a little water," scoffed Joe. "Are you afraid to get—"

All at once a thick column of water burst out of the hole, hitting Joe so hard it knocked him against the far wall of the chamber. He slumped to the ground, stunned. The water sprayed across his limp form, soaking his clothes and almost immediately filling the bottom of the chamber.

"Let me out of here!" Bill screamed. "We're going to drown!" He handed up the lantern and tried to pull himself over the edge of the hole. Frank reached in and helped him out.

"Where's Joe?" Frank shouted angrily. "You left him in there!"

"I don't care!" Bill shouted back, grabbing the rope and starting to climb out of the pit. Water dripped from his pants and shirt. "I'm getting out of here as fast as I can!"

Frank leaned over the hole and looked into the dark chamber that was rapidly filling with water. Frank quickly lowered himself into the chamber, landing in water that was nearly up to his thighs. There was no sign of his brother.

"Joe!" he shouted. "Where are you?"

But there was no answer.

7 The Seawater Tunnel

I've got to find Joe, Frank thought desperately.

He stooped down in the near darkness of the chamber as water sprayed wildly all around him and thrust his arms under the surface. When he felt his hands touch wet fabric, he grabbed hold of it and pulled upward. His brother's shirt appeared and then his brother inside it. Joe Hardy gasped, sputtered, and spit water out of his mouth.

"Ugh!" he grunted, then coughed loudly. "Wha— What happened?"

"You almost drowned!" Frank shouted above the roar of the water. "Come on! We've got to get out of here. This place is filling up!"

"Okay, okay," said Joe blearily.

"This way," Frank said, half dragging Joe toward

the opening above them. "Through this hole! Get moving. The water's already up to our waists."

"I'm moving!" said Joe, getting his senses back.

Frank grabbed his brother under the arms and lifted him toward the entrance to the chamber so Chet and George could pull him out the rest of the way. Then, with Joe out of the chamber, Frank let Chet and George haul him out, too.

By that time water had nearly filled the chamber below. Soon, it would begin to flow into the pit.

Bill was already out of the treasure pit, and George was scaling the rope. Joe grabbed the rope and began climbing, with Chet and Frank following close on his heels.

Once at the top, the group gathered around the treasure pit and looked down at the rising water beneath them.

"I don't believe this," said Frank. "The whole pit's filling with water. Where's it coming from?"

"Yuck!" said Joe, making a face. "I feel like I've swallowed a gallon of salt." He snapped his fingers. "Hey, that water must have been salt water— seawater!"

"Huh?" said Frank. "What would seawater be doing down there?"

"It's almost up *here*," said Chet, pointing into the pit. It was nearly half filled with water—and the water level was still rising.

"I think I know where this water is coming

from," said Damien. "That hole you found in the wall of the chamber—which side of the pit was it on?"

Joe tapped his foot on the edge of the pit. "I think it was right here," he said. "Of course, I may have gotten a little turned around down there."

"Is that correct?" Damien asked Bill.

"I guess so," Bill said. "Why the big deal?"

"I'll show you in a moment," Damien said. He pulled a small compass from his pocket and stared at it. "East by southeast," he said. "Approximately one hundred degrees." He turned to the others. "Let's take a look at the beach."

Damien led them across the clearing, around a clump of trees, and down to the pebble-covered beach. Once they had reached the beach, he pointed to the south and said, "This way."

Joe looked at Frank. "What's Professor Damien up to?" he asked.

Frank shrugged. "I don't know," he said. "But he seems to know what he's doing."

After twenty yards, the beach came to a dead end, blocked by a mound of boulders and dirt. Damien stared at the mound as though he were trying to see inside it.

"Looks like we can't go any farther, Professor," said Frank. "What do we do now?"

Damien thought for a moment. "We go into the water," he said finally.

"Not again!" Chet protested.

"I think what I'm looking for is this way," said the professor. He plunged into the surf without bothering to take off his shoes. "Well?" he said, when he noticed that the others weren't following. "Are you coming or not?"

"Why not?" said George, with a shrug. He waded into the water.

"I'm getting used to taking a swim with my clothes on," said Joe, rolling up his pants legs.

Reluctantly, the others splashed into the waves after George and the professor. The mound of boulders and dirt continued a short distance into the water, and Damien made his way haltingly around it. At the seaward end of the mound a thicket of vines and shrubs grew out of cracks in the rocks. The professor tore at the shrubs, ripping away limbs and vines and tossing them into the sea. The others stared at him as though he had gone crazy.

"Aha!" he cried finally. "Just as I thought!"

"Am I missing something?" asked Joe. "What are you talking about, Professor?"

"A cave!" Damien declared. "Behind this shrubbery! Help me clear an entrance."

He began tearing away more vegetation. The others pitched in. Within minutes they had exposed a dark opening in the side of the mound. The professor took the lantern and held it inside the opening.

"Follow me," he said. "Let's take a closer look."

"Oh, no," said Bill. "Not me. The last time I took a closer look at something, I almost got drowned."

"You almost let *me* drown, you mean!" said Joe.

"It was every man for himself down there, kid," Bill retorted.

Joe's eyes flashed. "Thanks a lot, you—" he began angrily. Then he felt the pressure of Frank's hand on his arm.

"Come on," Frank said quickly. "I want to see what's in that cave."

"Me, too," said Chet.

"Yeah, okay," muttered Joe. "Let's go."

"We'll wait here for you," George said, speaking for his companions.

Holding the lantern aloft, the professor plunged into the cave, followed by Frank, Joe, and Chet. The walls were narrow and wet. The surf flowed freely in and out of the cave, and the floor was covered by about two feet of water.

The cave was only about ten feet deep. As they proceeded, the professor, Chet, and the Hardys could hear a distinct gurgling sound, like water going down a drain.

"I knew it!" the professor said. "Here it is!" He lowered the lantern to the floor. The water poured

66

into a hole carved into the stone wall at the rear of the cave. "This is the source of the water," he said. "This is what flooded the pit."

"But how did the water get from here to there?" asked Joe.

"Someone went to a lot of trouble to dig a passageway," said Damien. "Obviously, there's a tunnel carrying the water from the surf to the pit. A seawater tunnel."

"But why?" asked Frank. "Why would somebody want to flood the pit?"

"Because something very important is buried at the bottom of it," said Damien. "I don't know what. But someone has gone to a great deal of trouble to protect whatever's down there."

"Who would have done it?" asked Joe. "Pirates?"

"Possibly," Damien answered. "The workmanship on this water tunnel is pretty crude. It's ingenious, though. Seventeenth century, perhaps. Pirates are certainly not out of the question."

"But if this was built in the seventeenth century, why did it flood now, hundreds of years later?" asked Frank.

"I think you broke a pressure seal," said Damien.

"A what?" asked Chet.

"That metal door we opened," said Damien. "I suspect it was designed to seal air in to the chamber.

When we forced open the door, we broke the seal—and let the air out of the chamber."

"What does that have to do with the water?" asked Joe.

"The air was keeping the water out of the chamber," said Damien. "When the air escaped, the water was able to flow in."

"I don't get it," said Chet. "How can air keep water out?"

"Imagine a straw inserted in a glass of water," Damien explained. "If you place your finger over the end of the straw as you insert it, the air in the straw is unable to escape and the water can't enter the straw. When you remove your finger, letting the air escape, the water flows into the straw all at once. When we opened the metal door, we were, in effect, taking our finger off the 'straw'—and the water flowed in."

"So what do we do now?" asked Frank. "The pit's full of water. We can't dig any more."

"We'll pump the water out," said Damien. "It shouldn't be too difficult, but we'll need to return to Bayport now for more equipment."

The professor led the way out of the cave. The three workmen were standing outside, with their arms crossed and bored looks on their faces.

"So what did you find?" asked Bill. "Captain Blackbeard and his merry men?"

"Nothing so trite," Damien said evenly. "Just a little mechanical marvel from ages past."

Bill Drake looked puzzled. "What are you talking about? What mechanical marvel?"

"Don't worry about it, Bill," said Joe. "You guys just do the muscle work and leave the stuff that requires brains to us, okay?"

"Why, you little—!" Bill growled, sloshing through the water toward Joe.

"Break it up!" said Frank, stepping between them. "The professor says we have to head back to Bayport."

The group made its way back to the beach. Once ashore, they returned to the pit, where they stacked their equipment in piles alongside the excavation. The seawater had risen to only a few feet below the top of the hole, roughly even with the seawater lapping at the beach.

"The water won't go any higher," said Damien. "It's high tide now. When the tide goes out, the water in the pit should drop, though not very much. However, the outgoing tide should expose the tunnel in the cove, giving us an opportunity to block it up."

"Are we going to come back after we get the equipment?" asked Frank.

Damien shook his head. "It's already late afternoon, and Mr. Kingsley is expecting us back at the marina soon. I'll round up the necessary supplies in Bayport this evening, then we'll return in the morning. Our equipment should be safe here overnight."

"Then let's get out of here," said Chet. "I'm ready for dinner."

"You're *always* ready for dinner," said Joe.

"That's not true," said Chet. "Sometimes I'm ready for lunch. Or breakfast."

"Or the ever-popular between-meals snack," added Joe.

"That, too," said Chet.

"Just be careful not to step in any quicksand on the way back to the ship," Frank told Joe.

"Hey, don't worry about me," said Joe. "I've learned my lesson. Watch your own step."

The wet and weary group trudged back into the woods. The Hardys and Chet walked together, the three workmen walked several feet apart, and Professor Damien trotted briskly ahead of them, apparently lost in his own thoughts.

"The quicksand was over there," said Frank, "so we'd better head this way." He pointed to the west.

"Fine with me," said Joe. "I can't wait to get home and get into some clean, dry clothes."

"You and me both," agreed Frank. "Wait till Mom, Dad, and Aunt Gertrude— Hey!"

Frank stumbled forward, his feet catching a taut

wire stretched between two trees. When he tripped, the wire snapped. As he fell, Frank looked up in time to see a plank of wood studded with nails falling out of the tree above him. It was heading straight for his head!

8 Deeper and Deeper

"Watch out!" shouted Joe, lunging frantically at his brother. He knocked Frank aside just as the spiked board whizzed past him. It struck the ground with a heavy thump and drove its sharp nails straight into the dirt.

"Wha—?" Frank gasped, rolling over and staring at the heavy board that lay next to him. "If that thing had hit me . . .!"

"You'd look like a well-used dart board," Chet said grimly, prying the board from the ground. "This thing weighs half a ton."

"Let me see that," said Frank, stumbling back to his feet. He took the board from Chet and examined it. It was a thick piece of gray wood through which about a dozen rusty nails had been hammered so that they stuck out the other side. "Is this another old pirate trap, Professor?"

Damien stroked his beard and stared at the board. "Not likely," he said.

"Then who put it there?" asked Chet.

"Someone out to cause a little mischief?" suggested the professor.

"Or somebody who doesn't like Frank, Chet, and me," said Joe. "I wonder who that could be." He turned to stare meaningfully at George, Jack, and Bill.

"Relax, kid," said George, puffing thoughtfully on a fresh cigar. "We're not out to get you, just to do a job and get paid."

"Yeah," added Bill. "And if I'd set that thing up, it wouldn't have missed."

"That really puts my mind at ease," Joe said sarcastically.

"There's no point in carrying on like this," Damien interrupted bluntly. "The trap could be left over from someone else's visit to the island. Maybe it was used by hunters."

"Hunters?" said Frank. "What kind of sick hunter would use a board covered with nails to kill an animal?"

Damien shrugged. "The world is full of strange people," he said.

"I'll say," said Joe, casting a last glance at the trio of workmen.

Twenty minutes later, the group was back on the boat. The cabin cruiser pulled out of the narrow harbor, with Damien at the helm. The Hardys stood at the front end of the boat while the workmen once again congregated in the rear. Chet was standing by the controls, talking to the professor, but they fell silent as news of Hurricane Celia crackled from the radio. To the relief of thousands of North Carolinians, it had turned out to sea. When the weather report was over, Damien used the shortwave radio to call ashore and let their sponsors know that they were returning.

Joe leaned on the railing and stared glumly out at the bay.

"What's eating you?" said Frank.

"I was really looking forward to this treasure-hunt business," answered Joe. "And now somebody's trying to spoil it."

"By trying to get us hurt?" said Frank. "Yeah, that would spoil it for me."

"Right," said Joe. "The seawater tunnel may have been built by a seventeenth-century pirate, but that spiked board was intended for one of *us.*"

"Why would somebody go so far to get rid of us?" asked Frank.

"Isn't it obvious?" Joe said. "So that he can have the treasure all to himself. We're here to protect Hurd's interests and make sure he gets his share of the treasure. But if something happens to us . . ."

". . . the others get to keep the treasure to themselves," finished Frank. "So who do you think's getting greedy?"

Joe shrugged. "I don't know, but let's keep our eyes on our friends over there. If they try anything funny, we'll let them have it."

"Let them have what?" Frank asked.

"We'll think of something," said Joe.

When the boat pulled into Kingsley Marina, Hurd Applegate was waiting on the dock. He waved the Hardys aside as soon as they came ashore.

"Well?" he asked, waving his cane excitedly. "What about the treasure? Did you find it?"

"Give us a break, Mr. Applegate," said Joe. "We've had only one day to look for it."

"We may be getting close, though," said Frank. "And whatever we're getting close to is valuable enough that somebody went to a lot of trouble to booby-trap it with water."

"Booby-trap?" asked a perplexed Hurd.

"Yeah," said Joe. "You'd have to see it to believe it. We almost drowned."

"You two *are* a mess," the older man said, stepping back to look at them. "You could use a change of clothes, that's for sure."

"Thanks," said Frank. "The thought has entered our minds, too."

Just then, someone drove a limousine into the

marina and parked it in the gravel lot. Vernon Prescott got out and joined the group on the dock.

"I got your message," he said to Damien. "What's this about you needing extra equipment?"

"We've had a small problem at the site," Damien told him. "We'll need a pump to remove water from the dig and some additional equipment to plug up a leak. I'll give you a list of what we need."

"A leak?" asked Prescott, with the same perplexed look Hurd had given the Hardys a moment before. "A pump? What kind of mess are you people getting yourselves into?" He turned to his three workmen. "What about you guys? Is everything fair and square?"

"So far, Mr. Prescott," George replied. "I'll give you a full report back in your office."

Joe gave Frank a meaningful look. "I'd like to be a fly on the wall when they give this 'report,' " he said in a low voice.

"Speaking of reports," said Damien, "where's Mr. Kingsley? I promised I'd let him know how things are going when I got back."

"I haven't seen him since this morning," Prescott said. "But I'm sure he'll be around soon. He owns this marina, after all."

As if in response to Damien's question, a large cabin cruiser sailed into the marina and pulled into a slip at the far end of the dock. Barrett Kingsley, wearing sturdy boating clothes, stood at the helm. A young man from the boathouse helped to moor his boat, then Kingsley joined the group.

"I'm sorry I'm late," he said with a broad smile, "but I couldn't resist taking a turn around the bay. Beautiful afternoon for boating, isn't it?" He stared more closely at the group. "You fellows look like you've had a rough day. What happened?"

Before Professor Damien could launch into his report of the day's events, Frank said, "Look, if nobody minds, Joe, Chet, and I are going to head on home. Meet you back here at nine A.M., Professor Damien?"

"We should be ready to cast off by then," the professor told them. "Get a good night's sleep. You'll need it."

Frank and Joe climbed into their van with Chet and drove home, dropping Chet off on the way. When they walked into their house, their aunt Gertrude raised her hand to her mouth in horror.

"You boys!" she said, gasping. "Whatever have you done to yourselves?"

Frank looked at his brother's badly stained clothing and then down at his own mud-spattered pants and T-shirt.

"Nothing that a couple of loads of laundry and a hot shower won't cure, Aunt Gertrude," he said with a grin.

"And the bad news," said Joe, as the brothers hurried up the stairs to their rooms, "is that we'll be doing it again tomorrow."

At nine the next morning, Frank, Joe, and Chet arrived at the marina, their T-shirts and pants freshly washed and ironed. Prescott's three burly workmen were loading a large contraption, which looked like an overgrown version of the sump pump that the Hardys kept in their basement, into the rear of the cabin cruiser.

"Do you think that'll pump out the pit?" asked Chet.

"It looks like it could pump out the whole bay," Joe said jokingly.

When the pump was loaded and everyone was on board, Damien piloted the cabin cruiser back out into Barmet Bay and toward Granite Cay. When they arrived at the island, Frank and Joe grabbed one side of the pump, Jack Kruger and Bill Drake the other, and they carried it ashore. Chet and George followed with a pair of rubber tubes that Damien had also placed on board the boat.

Fifteen minutes later, they were all back at the pit, setting up the pump. They ran one of the tubes into the pit itself and the other one down to the beach. Damien pressed a button on the side of the pump, and it began chugging loudly. The water level in the pit began dropping almost immediately as thick brown water gushed out of the tube and into the Atlantic.

While the pump was working, Damien took the Hardys back to the ship, where they retrieved a sack of powdered cement and some tools.

"What's this for?" Joe asked.

"We have to caulk up the seawater tunnel," said Damien. "There's no point in bailing out the pit if it simply fills up again every time the tide comes in."

Damien led the Hardys to the beach and into the hidden cave they had discovered the previous day. The entrance to the seawater tunnel was now completely empty of water.

"Just as I thought," said Damien. "Low tide. We won't have any more trouble until the tide rises again, and by then we should have it sealed."

Following Damien's instructions, the Hardys created a gooey mixture of seawater, powdered cement, and pebbles from the beach, which they used to build a makeshift dam across the entrance to the tunnel.

"When that hardens," said Damien, "it should prevent any water from entering the tunnel. We'll come back and check when the pumping is finished."

Pumping out the pit took about two hours. When the Hardys checked the cement dam again, it seemed to be holding up. Damien ordered the digging to begin again.

The treasure pit was a mess. The sides and bottom of the pit had turned into dark, wet mud that smelled of dead fish and seaweed.

"Yuck!" exclaimed Chet. "I'm not going back in there."

"I'm not going in there, either," said Bill Drake. "What if there's a cave-in or a mudslide while we're digging?"

"That's not likely," said Damien. "I've dug plenty of excavations in my career, and plenty of them have flooded. Not one of them has ever collapsed on me. Anyway, it's nearly noon and the sun is shining straight into the pit. The mud should dry in about an hour. We can wait until then to start digging."

An hour later, the pit was still muddy, but the smell was fading and the mud was drier and harder than it had been before. Convinced by Professor Damien that it was safe to go back in, the diggers tossed their picks and shovels into the pit and climbed down the rope.

"The first thing we're going to have to do," said Frank, "is get rid of this piece of metal." He tapped his shovel on the metal door that sealed the entrance to the flood chamber. The shovel made a hollow ringing sound as it hit the metal.

"Right," said Chet. "It's just getting in our way now."

The metal door was mounted in a wooden frame-

80

work that extended into the walls of the pit, keeping the roof of the flood chamber from collapsing. The treasure hunters dismantled the framework and sent the parts back up in the bucket. Then they lowered themselves into the chamber and broke up what remained of its earthen ceiling. When they were done, they began digging again.

With the added depth of the flood chamber, the pit was now over sixteen feet deep. But the heavy mud slowed down the digging, and by late afternoon there was still no sign of the treasure. Finally, Professor Damien signaled they should quit for the day.

George and Bill scaled the rope to the top, followed by Frank and Chet. Joe brought up the rear.

"Get moving, Hardy," shouted Chet from above as Joe neared the top of the pit. "My mom's got a big dinner waiting back in Bayport. You guys are invited. Of course, if you don't show up, I'll just have to eat it all by myself."

"Forget it," said Joe. "Next to Aunt Gertrude, your mom is the best cook in Bayport. And right now, I'm as hungry as you are all the time."

Joe was almost at the top when he felt himself slip. Looking up, he saw that the rope was fraying badly where it crossed the edge of the pit and that only a slender thread was still supporting his weight.

He glimpsed a discarded pick lying on the floor of the pit. The point was aimed directly at him. With a chill of terror, Joe realized that if he didn't make it to the top before the thread broke, he was going to fall onto the sharp point of the pick— almost twenty feet below!

9 Marooned!

For two or three long seconds, Joe froze in place, afraid that if he kept moving he would cause the rope to fray even faster. Below, the upturned pick pointed toward him like an arrow aimed at his heart.

"Hey, Joe!" shouted Chet. "Why'd you stop climbing?"

Joe snapped out of his horrified trance. "Give me a hand!" he shouted. "The rope's about to break!"

"What are you—?" Chet knelt down and his eyes fell on the fraying thread. "Uh-oh! You *are* in trouble!"

Chet grabbed Joe's wrist. At that moment, the thread snapped and suddenly Chet was supporting all of Joe's weight with his one hand. Chet quickly grabbed Joe's other wrist and gripped it tightly—but Joe was far too heavy for him to pull out.

"He-e-e-e-elp!" Chet shouted. "Somebody grab me before he pulls *me* in!"

Frank dived to the rescue, throwing his muscular bulk on top of Chet to prevent him from sliding after Joe. He reached over the top of Chet's head and grabbed one of Joe's wrists. Together Frank and Chet pulled Joe to the edge of the pit, where he could grab hold of the ground and pull himself up the rest of the way.

"Good work, Chet," Joe gasped as he crawled back onto the ground. "You saved my life. You, too, Frank."

Frank stared over the edge of the pit and gave a low whistle. "I see what your problem was," he said to his brother. "Somebody's pick was waiting down there to skewer you."

"I don't understand how this could have happened," said Damien. "That rope was sturdy enough to last for months."

Joe pulled the broken end of the rope out of the pit. "I'm not convinced this was an accident," he said.

"What are you talking about?" asked Frank.

"Look at these marks on the rope," Joe said, pointing. "It looks like somebody's cut it about halfway through. Only half of it looks frayed."

"I see what you mean," Frank said, nodding.

84

"Somebody cut the rope, then the weight of everybody climbing on it finished the job. By the time you got to the top, it was ready to snap."

"You got it," said Joe. "And since the cut was on the underside of the rope, nobody noticed it until it was too late." Joe's eyes narrowed and a look of anger passed over his face. "All of which means that somebody tried to kill me."

"Not just you," Frank countered. "Chet and I were just ahead of you on that rope."

"But who could have done it?" asked Chet. "Who would have had a chance?"

"I don't know," said Frank. "Did you see anyone near the rope, Professor?"

"No," Damien replied, "but I was down at the beach much of the time, making sure that our cement dam was holding properly."

"Jack Kruger was near the rope," said Joe. "He was hauling the buckets up and down. He had plenty of opportunity to cut it."

The muscular workman stared at Joe. "Are you accusing me of cutting that rope?" he asked in his deep, rumbling voice.

"I'm saying that this looks pretty suspicious," said Joe. "Maybe you guys and Vernon Prescott have some sort of plan going that'll let you keep this treasure for yourselves. And maybe that's why this rope got cut and why that board was in that tree yesterday afternoon."

"Take it easy, Joe," cautioned Frank. "Don't jump to conclusions."

Kruger moved toward Joe menacingly. "You talk big for a little boy," he said. "Do you want to start a fight?"

Joe looked Kruger straight in the eye. "I'll save it for later," he said. "That's because I'm a *big* boy."

"Good thinking," said Frank, pulling Joe aside. "You don't want to start making unproven accusations against these guys, at least until we've got some kind of evidence."

"But next time they might try to kill you or Chet," said Joe angrily, clenching his fists. "If Kruger's the one who cut that rope, we're all in danger."

"We don't have any proof that it was him," said Frank. "We'll just have to be careful."

Joe finally unclenched his fists. "Oh, all right," he said grudgingly. "But don't think I won't have my eyes on you!" he snapped, turning back to Kruger.

The big man shrugged and walked away. Bill Drake looked at Joe and laughed.

"Listen to this!" cried Damien suddenly.

He was holding the transistor radio. A staticky voice was reading a weather forecast over the air in urgent tones:

". . . has unexpectedly turned back toward shore and is expected to strike coastal regions sometime

86

this evening. A travel advisory is in effect for the entire Bayport area, and all oceangoing traffic is advised to put ashore until further notice. The storm, Hurricane Celia, is believed to be the worst to approach the Atlantic coastal region in nearly twenty years. . . ."

"What?" blurted Joe. "Hurricane Celia? I thought we heard that it had gone out to sea or something."

"We did," said Frank. "It must have changed course. It's a good thing we're heading back to Bayport."

"Yes," said Damien. "And we'd better get there as soon as possible. They must have been broadcasting this warning all day, but we never heard it. Unfortunately, there's no time to carry our gear back to the boat. We'll lower another rope into the pit and use it to place our gear in the bottom, where it will be safe from the winds. Then we'll cover the pit with a tarpaulin so it won't flood. We can weight the tarpaulin down with the pump to keep it from blowing away. I just hope our little concrete dam in the seawater tunnel remains in place when the waves hit."

The group hurried to follow the archaeologist's orders. When they were finished, the pit was sealed off and the equipment shut up inside.

The seven cautiously made their way back through the woods. When they reached the far side of the island, they stumbled out of the trees and down to the beach.

But there was nothing waiting for them.

"Where's the boat?" cried Chet.

"It's gone!" said George. "Vanished!"

"It has to be somewhere around here," said Frank, scrambling up the steep, dirt-covered hill that led to the top of the granite cliff looming over the harbor. At the top, Frank crawled onto the flat surface of the rock and stared out into the bay.

Then he saw it. About a quarter of a mile away, in the middle of the sparkling late-afternoon waters, was the cabin cruiser.

Frank could see no one on board, but the boat was speeding away from them, right into the middle of Barmet Bay!

10 The Fire Pit of the Uzca

"There's the boat!" cried Frank, pointing toward the water. "It's heading away from us into the bay!"

He scrambled back down the rock and stood beside his brother.

"What are we going to do now?" Joe asked.

"We'll have to radio for help," said Bill.

"The only two-way radio was on the boat," Damien reminded them.

"Somebody will come looking for us," said George Lewin. "Mr. Prescott and the others know we're here."

"By the time they're sure we're missing," Joe said, "the hurricane will have hit, and nobody will be able to get a boat into the bay."

"Just what I needed," moaned Bill. "To be stuck on an island with some loudmouthed kids!"

"This is terrible," said Damien in an agitated tone. "Without the boat, we'll still be here when the storm arrives. We'll have to find some sort of shelter."

"What about a cave?" asked Frank. "Like the one with the seawater tunnel in it."

"If there were other caves here, they might make satisfactory shelter, but I haven't seen any and there's no time to look," Damien said. "And the cave with the seawater tunnel is on the windward side of the island, facing directly into the Atlantic. That is, directly into the hurricane. No. We have to stay on the lee side of the island—the side away from the wind—and hope for the best. Maybe the trees will serve as a windbreak."

"What about this beach?" said Joe.

"The beach would be too exposed," said Frank. "We're right on the water."

"That isn't necessarily a problem," said Damien. "The storm will be coming from the east, out of the ocean. This beach faces into the bay and offers us the maximum shelter, with the entire island between us and the storm."

"We could take shelter under the cliff," suggested Frank.

"No," said Damien. "That might be *too* close to

the water. There will be high waves, regardless of the direction of the wind. But there are a couple of places where the beach penetrates some distance from the shore, right up to the edge of the woods."

"Then we can dig a trench in the beach," suggested Joe. "Frank and I will get a couple of shovels and build a makeshift shelter."

Twenty minutes later Frank and Joe returned with a pair of shovels. Taking turns with the others, they dug a deep trench in the pebbles and sand of the beach, with both sides protected by high piles of dirt.

Above them, thick gray clouds were gathering, streaming eastward over the island and blotting out the sky. The wind picked up, and the trees in the forest began to sway back and forth. Joe felt a twinge of apprehension as he watched the first signs of the gathering storm.

"Keep your fingers crossed," said Frank, as he dug. "Maybe it will change course again."

"Somehow I don't think we're going to be that lucky," said Joe.

By the time full darkness had arrived, it was obvious that they were *not* going to be lucky. The wind grew fiercer, and the sky became increasingly cloudy. There was a sharp smell of rain in the air, and flashes of lightning were visible in the sky above the bay.

Let it be a mild storm, thought Joe. Let it blow itself out somewhere in the middle of the Atlantic Ocean, not in the middle of Barmet Bay.

The treasure hunters gathered in the narrow trench they had dug in the beach. The Hardys and Chet huddled at one end, while Prescott's workmen gathered nervously at the other. Damien paced back and forth, anxiously staring at the sky.

"I can't stand this waiting," said Chet. "The sooner the storm comes, the sooner it'll be over."

"Why don't we tell ghost stories or something?" Joe said.

"What about a pirate story?" suggested Frank. "How about it, Professor? You're the expert."

Damien stopped his pacing and sat down. "Well, I suppose I might have a tale to tell."

"Oh, goody!" Bill said mockingly. "A bedtime story."

"Take it easy, Bill," said George, laying a hand on his companion's shoulder.

"History has a lot to teach us," said Damien. "It's important to take it seriously."

"Did a lot of pirates visit this area?" asked Frank.

Damien nodded. "Quite a few. The seventeenth century was the age of the pirate, but it's often difficult to determine who was where, and when. Pirates rarely kept records of their voyages, since those records could be used against them in court, should they run afoul of the law."

"I'd think a pirate would run afoul of the law all the time," said Joe.

"Not necessarily," said Damien. "Many pirates were actually privateers, under government commission to harass enemy ships in time of war. And besides, pirates were often very popular with townspeople because they brought trade goods with them—never mind that they had taken the goods by force or stolen them outright. Upstanding citizens often ignored little details like that, especially when the pirates offered a good price for what they were selling."

An unusually loud gust of wind blew through the trees above their heads. Chet, Joe, and Frank looked up at the sky for a minute with worried expressions on their faces. Then they turned back to Professor Damien.

"So what seventeenth-century pirates do you think visited Bayport?" asked Chet.

"Better still," asked Frank, "which ones might have buried treasures here?"

"Well," said Damien, "Captain Kidd may have left a few treasures around. But if I had to guess who the treasure of Granite Cay might have belonged to, I'd bet on Henry Dafoe."

"I've never heard of him," said Frank.

"Me, neither," said Joe.

"I haven't heard of him, either," said Chet.

"Well, he may have been the most important

pirate of all," said Damien. "But he was little known to the general public in his time and not much is known about him today."

"So who *was* this Dafoe guy?" asked Frank.

"He was a pirate who sailed under the Dutch flag. He spent most of his career in the Caribbean, although he sailed north occasionally. He even made a trip into the South American jungles once, an ambitious journey for a pirate, since it took him far from the sea. He was rumored to have captured one of the greatest treasures of all, but no one knows what he did with it."

Twin forks of lightning suddenly shot through the sky overhead, followed seconds later by the sharp crackling of thunder.

"What kind of treasure was it?" asked Joe, trying to ignore the thunder.

"The treasure trove of the Uzca," said Damien, so wrapped up in his own story that he seemed to be unaware of the lightning. "They were one of the largest Indian nations in South America. They lived in what is now the country of Costa de Oro."

"Wow!" said Chet. "What was the treasure made of? Gold? Silver?"

"It's hard to say for sure," replied Damien. "Probably jewelry, gemstones that had been plundered by the Uzca over the centuries. They were a warlike tribe and took a lot of prizes in battle. The centerpiece of the treasure, though, was supposedly the Green Star of the Amazon."

"The Green Star of the Amazon?" Joe repeated, raising his voice so that it could be heard over the howling of the wind.

"It was a perfect emerald, possibly the largest ever known," said Damien. "According to the legend, Dafoe plucked the Green Star from the Uzca fire pit itself."

Chet shivered, partly from the wind and partly from the eeriness of Damien's story. "The Uzca fire pit? That sounds really neat."

" 'Neat' is the word for it," Damien said dryly. "The legend says that the Uzca had placed the Green Star at the bottom of a deep cavern, where it was used on special ceremonial occasions."

"What kind of ceremonies?" asked Frank.

Damien hesitated for a moment. "Maybe I shouldn't tell you," he said finally.

"Hey," said Joe. "That's not fair! Now you've got my curiosity up."

"Mine, too," said Chet.

"You can't stop now, Professor," said Frank.

"No," said Joe, looking up nervously at the dark clouds racing across the sky. "But the wind might drown him out."

"Well, all right, I'll tell you," said Damien. "The ceremonies of the Uzca involved human sacrifice.

The legend says that Dafoe himself was captured and brought to the fire pit to be sacrificed."

"Why was it called the fire pit?" asked Joe.

"The high priests of the Uzca had built an altar on which they placed the Green Star. Surrounding the altar was a ring of firewood. Then they set the wood afire to keep anyone from approaching the stone. They tied Dafoe to a stake in the middle of the pit, where he was to be burned alive."

"Ouch!" said Chet. "What a way to go."

"Did he get away?" asked Frank.

"Unfortunately, the legend grows a little unclear at this point. But one version says that the high priests had indeed set fire to the kindling at Dafoe's feet, and the flames were roaring upward when—"

Cra-a-a-a-ck!

All at once the sky seemed to burst open. Multiple streaks of lightning filled the heavens, and a single bolt of lightning struck the beach itself, no more than fifty feet from the trench. The professor's final words were lost in the explosion of light and sound.

"Here it comes!" shouted Joe, unable to hear his own voice above the sounds of the storm.

A torrent of wind-driven rain swept across the trench where the Hardys and their companions sat huddled, pelting them like a volley of liquid bullets. Frank raised his arms as if they would protect him from the cloudburst, but the rain soaked his clothes almost instantly, and after that there hardly seemed to be a point in trying to protect himself.

"How long do you think this will last?" Frank shouted to Damien.

"What?" replied Damien, holding a dripping hand to his wet ear. "I can't hear you."

"How long?" repeated Frank, pointing to his wristwatch in pantomime. "The storm."

Damien shrugged. "At least an hour," he shouted. "Maybe until morning."

There was another crackling noise from overhead. Frank looked up, expecting to see another multiforked lightning bolt sizzling over the treetops. But to his horror he saw something else.

One of the tallest trees in the forest was leaning directly over the trench, its trunk badly splintered. Suddenly, the trunk gave way and the tree began to fall.

"Look out!" screamed Frank.

He grabbed Joe and Chet and pushed them out of the way just in time. The tree smashed across the trench in the spot where they had been sitting seconds earlier.

"That was close," yelled Frank, his voice trembling with relief.

"I'll say," shouted Joe. He looked around. "Where's Professor Damien?"

"He was right next to us," shouted Chet.

Frank stared at Joe in horror. "I didn't see him move away, did you?"

"I think I've found him," said Chet, his voice shaking and barely audible in the storm. He pointed toward the fallen tree.

Professor Damien was lying in the trench, his face twisted in pain. The lower part of his body was trapped beneath the bulk of the fallen tree!

11 An Unexpected Guest

Underneath the fallen tree limb, the professor was mouthing the words, "Help me!"

"We've got to lift the tree!" Frank shouted. He signaled desperately to the trio of workmen, who were already making their way toward Damien.

"You guys grab that side of the tree, we'll take this one," Frank yelled.

Jack Kruger nodded and stooped to grab the tree in his massive arms. The other workmen did the same. Frank, Chet, and Joe lifted from the other side.

At first the tree refused to budge, but then they were able to move it slowly upward. The professor, grimacing in pain, wriggled his way out from underneath. When he was completely clear, Frank and the others let the tree drop.

"Whew!" said Joe. "Are you all right, Professor?"

Damien nodded as he gingerly felt his legs and feet. "Nothing broken," he said, gasping, his voice audible during a brief lull in the wind. "I was lucky. I could have been killed."

"It could have been any of us," said Frank. He looked around to see Chet, Joe, and the workmen nodding their wet faces in agreement.

"I hope this hurricane ends soon," George said uneasily. "Who knows what could happen next."

But the storm took more than four hours to blow over. It finally ended in the early hours of the morning. As the last howling winds of the hurricane faded away, the seven treasure hunters were able to fall into an uncomfortable sleep, only to be awakened before six the next morning by the singing of birds. The sky was already bright blue and so clear that it was hard to believe such a ferocious storm had passed through only hours earlier.

"What a night," Joe said with a groan. "I feel like I slept in a cement mixer."

"Me, too," said Frank. "When we get home, I'm going to sleep for a week."

"*If* we get home," said Chet. "Do you think somebody'll come looking for us today?"

"I hope so," said Joe. "But the storm probably

caused a lot of other emergencies and they'll need to be taken care of first. It'll be a while before anybody gets on our trail."

"Mr. Prescott will come looking for us," said George. "He won't leave us marooned out here."

"He'd better not," growled Bill. "I'm going to demand triple pay for every extra minute I spend on this island."

"It might take Prescott a while to find a boat he can use to rescue us with," said Joe.

"Barrett Kingsley already has a boat," Chet reminded them. "Maybe he'll come and get us."

"That's true," said Frank. "He'll probably guess we got stuck here and come after us."

Professor Damien rose to his feet, wincing. "Well, I seem to have survived the storm," he said, "thanks to the rest of you. I don't know what I would have done without you." He glanced around. "Did anyone think to bring extra food, so that we can have some breakfast?"

"I did," said Chet. He pulled a large plastic-wrapped package from his knapsack.

"And knowing Chet, it's probably enough to feed a small army for a week," Joe said, with a grin.

"Well, we all need it," said Frank. "Even our friends over there"—he jerked his head in the direction of Prescott's workmen—"need some food if they're going to get any digging done today."

"Digging?" said Bill. "We're going to keep digging after what happened last night?"

"Why not?" said Joe. "We're stuck here. We might as well do something useful."

"My feelings exactly," said Professor Damien. "Let's make the best of a bad situation."

"By the way, Professor," said Frank, "whatever became of Henry Dafoe? Was he made into a sacrifice?"

"Well," said the archaeologist, "I hate to bring the story to such an anticlimax, but no one really knows. Dafoe's name turns up in a few later tales, but none of them are documented."

"What a disappointment!" said Chet. "That story really had me going. Now I feel like I rented a great movie and somebody chopped off the end of the tape."

Professor Damien smiled sympathetically at Chet. "I'm afraid that's the difference between movies and real life," he said. "History rarely provides tidy endings. Now, I suggest we parcel out our breakfast rations and prepare to resume digging."

Chet passed around his usual assortment of snacks—crackers, cheese dip, chocolate chip cookies, and raisins.

"I knew your appetite would come in handy one day," Joe teased.

"I can't believe I'm eating cheese dip for breakfast," George said, shaking his head.

"I think I have very good taste in food," Chet said, looking a little offended.

Frank had to smother a laugh as everyone else kept their eyes down and ate.

After breakfast, the treasure hunters headed for the pit. The tarpaulin, weighted down on one side by the heavy pump, had remained secure during the storm. When they reopened the pit, they found everything in order; the seawater dam had apparently held up and the interior of the pit was dry.

"Everybody grab a shovel," said Frank. "Let's get back to work."

Joe nudged Frank with his elbow. "Remember to keep your eye on those guys at all times," he whispered, indicating the workmen. "I wouldn't be surprised if they tried some more funny stuff today."

"How can I keep my eyes on those guys and dig for treasure at the same time?" asked Frank.

"You're a detective," Joe reminded him. "You're supposed to have eyes in the back of your head."

The professor and Jack Kruger rerigged the bucket-and-rope system while the others climbed into the pit. Five minutes later the digging had resumed.

"I'm getting sick of this digging," grumbled Bill

Drake. "That message we found said the treasure was twenty feet deep. We've dug at least that far. We should have found it by now. Unless the whiz kid here"—he jerked his thumb at Frank—"got the secret code wrong."

"If my brother says the message said twenty feet," snapped Joe, "then it said twenty feet."

Bill Drake's shovel made a sharp scraping sound. "Hey," he cried, "I've hit something. Maybe it's the treasure!"

"Or maybe it's just another doorway to nowhere," said George glumly.

"No," said Bill, bending down to scrape dirt away with his hand. "There's something here. Something hard. It's—"

He stood up abruptly, a look of horror on his face. Frank looked down to see what had shocked Bill. On the ground, next to Bill's shovel, lay an object that stared up at him from the dirt.

A human skull!

12 Dead Pirates

"Professor!" shouted Frank. "You'd better take a look at this!"

Professor Damien appeared at the mouth of the pit. "What's all the fuss about? Have you found something left behind by a pirate?"

"I think we found the pirate himself," said Joe. "Which may explain why he never came back for his treasure."

The professor peered over the edge of the pit. "I'm afraid my legs ache too much from my encounter with that tree to climb down to the bottom of this pit and take a closer look, but, yes, I see. Is there a skeleton connected to that skull?"

"I don't think I want to find out," said Bill Drake.

"Who wants to dig it up?" asked Joe.

"Not me," said Chet.

"I'm getting a blister on my shovel hand," said George. "Count me out."

"Don't be such babies," said Frank. "This is a real live pirate. I mean, a real *dead* one. I mean—you know what I mean."

Frank traded his shovel for a trowel and began digging around the skull. Joe knelt down and gave him a hand. After a half hour of work, with running instructions from Professor Damien, they had unearthed most of a human skeleton. The bones were a dingy gray and brown after being buried for centuries.

"He was a big guy," said Joe. "I'm glad I didn't meet him while he was alive."

"What's this?" said Chet, examining a piece of dirty metal lying next to the skeleton's neck. "It looks like a necklace of some kind."

"That's not a necklace," said Frank. "It's a chain."

Joe went to lift the chain off the ground, but it stuck. He quickly troweled around it, then told Frank, "One of those flagstones is attached to it."

Frank took the flagstone from his brother. "There's another coded message carved on it," he said.

"Think you can solve this one?" asked Joe.

"I don't see why not," said Frank, reaching into

106

his backpack to extract the sheet of paper he had used to decode the first message two days before. "Give me a minute." He pulled a pencil from his pocket and started to write on the paper.

"Got it," he said a few minutes later. "Look at this!" He handed the paper to Joe.

"Well?" the professor called impatiently.

" 'This is the fate,' " Joe read, " 'of any who come after my treasure. H. Dafoe.' "

"So this treasure really did belong to Dafoe," said Frank.

"Who do you think our thin friend might be?" said Joe, pointing at the skeleton.

"Probably one of Dafoe's diggers," said the professor. "An unfortunate pirate who helped him bury his treasure. The only way to guarantee that the whereabouts of treasure remained secret was to kill those who knew about it."

"This Dafoe was a real nice guy," said Chet.

"He was a pirate," Damien pointed out. "They weren't exactly known for their kind and gentle manners. You'll probably find other skeletons as you dig," added Damien. "It takes more than a few people to bury a treasure this deep. And this is probably where they were buried."

Even as Damien spoke, Chet's shovel struck another hard object. "I think I've found another skull," he said. "This is getting really spooky."

"Yeah," said Joe, looking at the first skeleton. "We're going to send these guys up to you in the bucket, Professor."

Frank and Joe gathered the bones of the first skeleton and piled them into the bucket. Jack Kruger hauled them up, and the professor removed them. Then Kruger lowered the bucket back into the pit.

Chet had indeed struck a second skeleton. As they were unearthing it, Bill Drake found a third and then a fourth. One by one, their bones were hauled up to Professor Damien.

"I hope that's all," said Chet.

"Yeah," said Joe. "It's crowded enough down here without all these dead pirates turning up."

George's shovel scraped against something hard. "Oh, no," said Chet. "Not another skeleton!"

George chomped on his cigar. "No," he said. "It feels like metal." He bent down and scraped away dirt with his hand, revealing a dark, metallic surface.

"Another door?" asked Joe.

"Maybe it's the lid of a chest," suggested Frank.

"Maybe it's the treasure!" cried Chet.

"You kids may be right," said George.

"Hurry up," said Frank, leaning heavily on his shovel. "Let's get this thing uncovered."

After a few minutes of digging, they had managed to reveal the entire chest. It was carved out of dark wood and was about three feet long and two feet high. The image of a skull and crossbones was etched into one side, and the initials *HD* were carved into the other. The lid had bronze hinges that had turned green with age.

"Open it," Chet said excitedly.

Joe bent down and tried to lift the lid. "It's locked," he said. "But there's a keyhole on the front."

"Terrific," said Frank. "Anybody bring a key?"

"How about a skeleton key," Chet said jokingly. Frank and Joe looked at him and rolled their eyes.

"I brought a drill you can use," said Professor Damien from the top of the pit. "I'll put it in the bucket and lower it down."

Jack Kruger hauled up the bucket, Damien dropped something heavy into it, and then the bucket was lowered again. Joe reached in and pulled out an old-fashioned hand-operated drill.

"I hope this thing can handle the job," Joe said. "It looks as old as the chest."

"Come on," Frank said, shaking his head. "Just do it."

"Yes, sir," said Joe. He began cranking the drill against the lid of the chest, next to the keyhole.

Flecks of wood and dirt flew into the air as Joe turned the handle of the drill. A musty smell filled the pit. Finally, the drill broke through the top of the chest.

"Got it!" cried Joe triumphantly.

"Good," said Frank. "Now what?"

"Now I try to open it," said Joe. He pulled on the top of the chest again. It wouldn't budge.

"No luck?" asked Frank.

"No luck," Joe said, sighing. "I guess I'll have to drill another hole."

"With you kids on the job," snapped Bill Drake, "we're never going to get that thing open. Let me do it."

"Wait," said Joe, leaning over the chest. "Let me try something."

He put his finger in the drilled hole and probed around inside the chest. He felt nothing, only empty space. Leaning closer, he put his eye next to the hole.

"Maybe I can see inside," he said. "Give me a second."

"What are you going to see?" said Bill. "It's probably dark in there."

"You never know," said Joe, bending down beside the chest. He moved his face toward the hole, trying to get a glimpse inside.

"I think I saw a flicker of light," said Joe. "No, it was a reflection off the keyhole. I sure can smell something, though. Yuck, it smells—"

Joe stopped in midsentence. Frank leaned toward him, wondering what it was that his brother had smelled and why he was frozen in place.

Suddenly Joe keeled over sideways and fell unconscious to the floor of the pit!

13 The Treasure Chamber

"Another trap!" cried Chet. "Joe, are you all right?"

"Of course he's not all right!" shouted Frank, shaking his brother to revive him. "Wake up, Joe! Say something!"

"That kid's out like a light," Bill observed. "I don't think he's going to say much."

Suddenly Frank, who was crouching right next to the chest, began to sway. Everything started spinning around.

"Hey, Professor!" shouted Chet. "We need help!"

Frank heard the professor's voice coming from the top of the pit. "Hold your breath and stay away from the chest," Damien shouted. "There must be chemicals inside which, combined with oxygen, form a poisonous gas. It should dissipate pretty soon. Just move Joe and Frank away from the chest until they've recovered."

Frank felt somebody lift him and prop him against the wall of the pit. He opened his eyes and saw Chet and George staring down at him. Chet was shaking him and speaking his name over and over again. Chet and George were also spinning around in circles, but soon the spinning began to slow down.

"What . . . what happened?" Frank mumbled.

"You got too close to the chest," Chet told him. "The professor thinks you got a whiff of poison gas."

"Ummm," moaned Joe, who was propped up against the opposite wall.

"I think the other kid's coming around, too," said George.

Joe shook his head and grimaced. "I feel lousy," he muttered.

Frank rubbed his head. "Who put poison gas in the chest? Our friend Henry Dafoe?"

"I think so," said Professor Damien from the top of the pit. "He must have been every bit as ruthless as legend says he was."

"That didn't stop him from leaving clues," said Frank. "Like the flagstones. He must have known somebody would come looking."

113

"It was a game to him," said the professor. "He was quite intelligent. He enjoyed matching wits with his enemies, leading them on and then lowering the boom."

"The gas is probably gone by now," said Damien. "You might try drilling again."

"You can handle it this time," said Joe to Frank.

"Thanks a lot," said Frank, picking up the drill. "If nobody minds, I'm going to hold my breath."

"Good idea," said Joe.

Frank squatted down beside the chest and placed the drill bit as close to the metal lock as he could.

Five minutes later, the drill broke through to the interior. Frank felt the lock come loose as he pulled the bit back out. "I think I've got it," he said. "It's ready to open."

Frank placed his hands on either side of the chest. His heart thumping wildly, he slowly raised the lid and leaned over to look inside. The light from above shone into the chest.

"I can't believe this!" Frank exclaimed. "The chest is empty!"

"Not again," Joe said in disgust. "I like this Dafoe guy less every minute."

"Now we have to do more digging!" groaned Chet.

They picked up their shovels and began digging again. But when nothing of interest had been found after two more hours, the treasure hunters began to get impatient.

"Hey, Professor," Frank finally said. "How about it? We're about ready to give up."

Damien looked stricken. "Please! Not yet! We may be very close to finding the treasure."

"I don't think I believe that message about its being 'twenty feet below,'" said George.

"It's just possible," the professor called from above, "that Dafoe's clues have sent us in the wrong direction."

"Direction!" said Frank, snapping his fingers. "That's it! We're going straight down, but maybe Dafoe went in a different direction!"

"Huh?" said Chet. "Where else could he have gone? Straight up?"

"No," said Frank, "but he could have gone slantwise, off at an angle. Of course, then we wouldn't have found those skeletons and the chest down here, but maybe Dafoe's pit was L-shaped. He could have gone straight down for a bit, then gone sideways, knowing that anybody who dug up the pit later would keep going straight."

"It's certainly a possibility," said Damien.

"Where would he have turned sideways?" asked Joe.

"At the twenty-foot mark," said Frank. "Exactly where his message said the treasure would be."

"So where's the twenty-foot mark?" asked Chet.

"Well," said Frank, "I'm six feet one, and we've gone down about twenty-five feet, so it should be about here." He held his hand at about shoulder level.

"Now all we have to do," said Joe, "is figure out what direction Dafoe went in."

"Look!" said Frank, pointing. "The dirt on this side of the pit is a different color from the dirt on the other sides."

"So what?" said Bill.

"So maybe somebody dug on this side a few hundred years ago," said Frank. "The dirt would be packed differently—and that would make it look different."

"What do we do now?" asked Chet.

"Flip the bucket upside down," said Frank. "I'll stand on top of it and dig into the wall of the pit. I can use the dirt I dig out to fill the bottom of the pit so that it will be easier to reach the hole."

Joe turned the bucket over, and Frank stood on it. He gripped his shovel halfway down the handle and jabbed it at the wall over and over again. Dirt came loose in clumps, raining down into the bottom of the pit.

All at once there was a crunching sound, as though Frank's shovel had struck rotting wood.

"I think I've found something!" said Frank excitedly.

116

The others began digging alongside him, knocking dirt and rotted wood out of the wall. Suddenly Chet's shovel broke through into an open space.

"There's some kind of opening here," said Chet.

"It looks like a boarded-up tunnel!" Joe exclaimed.

Working quickly, they removed the rest of the boards and the dirt, revealing a gaping black entranceway.

"Send down the lantern, Professor!" shouted Frank. "I'm going inside!"

"You're standing on the bucket," the professor replied. "Let me have it, and I'll lower the lantern to you."

Frank did as the professor suggested. Moments later, when the lantern had been lowered into the pit, Frank stood on the bucket again and peered through the hole. Strange flickering reflections shone back at him.

"What do you see?" Joe asked.

"I can't tell yet," Frank said excitedly. "Somebody give me a boost."

Chet and Joe grabbed Frank's legs and pushed him up. He placed the lantern on the ledge, grabbed the edges of the hole, and pulled himself through. Lifting his legs into the hole after him, he lay in the ancient tunnel and reached for the lantern. Only a few feet ahead of him, he could see a large underground chamber. For the first time in three hundred years, the chamber filled with light.

Frank gasped.

He stood and walked into the chamber, which was large enough to stand in. The walls were made of dirt and clay. Within them sat a collection of ancient artifacts more dazzling than anything Frank had ever seen in a museum.

There were bars of gold. Glittering jewels in every color of the rainbow. Gold and silver coins with the faces of forgotten kings carved on them. Jade statues of mythical animals. Weapons and armor fashioned from precious metals. And all of it seemed to gleam and sparkle in the dim light of the lantern that Frank held.

"What is it?" Joe shouted excitedly.

"You're not going to believe this," said Frank in awestruck tones. "Come on in and take a look!"

"I'm going in there," said Chet. "Here! Help me climb on the bucket."

Chet stepped onto the bucket and clambered his way into the hole. He was followed seconds later by Joe, then George and Bill. Even Jack Kruger, attracted by the excitement at the bottom of the pit, scaled his way down the rope and climbed through the hole.

Once inside the chamber, the six treasure hunters stood in silence and looked around, stunned by what they saw.

118

"The treasure of Henry Dafoe," Frank said finally. "It really exists."

Twenty feet above the treasure, the professor was shouting frantically. "Please! You've got to tell me what you found! I have to know!"

"Calm down, Professor," said Frank as he climbed out of the pit. "I'll tell you everything."

As Frank described what he had seen inside the treasure chamber, the professor's jaw fell open. His eyes widened in amazement, and his hands began to tremble.

"This—this is amazing!" he stammered. "The find of a lifetime! It—it must be the treasure trove of the Uzca. It was thought to be just a legend until now—but it actually exists! This is the greatest archaeological discovery since the tomb of Tutankhamen!"

"Well, I'm glad I could make your day, Professor," said Frank, smiling. He could understand why the archaeologist was so excited. "Hurd Applegate, Mr. Prescott, and Mr. Kingsley should be pretty happy about our find, too."

"Indeed," said the archaeologist shortly.

"Do you want to come down and take a look, Professor Damien?" Frank asked.

"I—I don't think I'm in good enough condition for the climb," he said distractedly. "I'm sorry, Frank, but this discovery is just too momentous. I

119

need some time to think . . . to plan. I'll be back in a moment."

"Sure, Professor," said Frank, as Damien wandered away from the pit.

"Well?" said Joe, poking his head through the hole. "How did the professor react?"

"I'm not sure," said Frank. "He seemed really excited, and then, when I mentioned Hurd and the others, he got upset and disappeared. I don't know why."

"Probably nothing to worry about," said Joe. "Come back in and look at this stuff. It's really incredible!"

Frank reentered the chamber and joined Chet, Joe, Jack, George, and Bill in rummaging through the centuries-old treasure of Henry Dafoe. Jack Kruger was polishing a dagger with an ivory handle and admiring his reflection in the metal blade. Bill Drake and George Lewin were sifting through a pile of gold coins, letting them fall to the floor and then picking them up again, like ancient kings admiring their treasures. Joe and Chet were examining the jewels.

Finally, when the dark, narrow chamber began to seem too stuffy, the six treasure hunters climbed back out into the pit.

"Where's the professor?" asked Chet, looking up.

"I don't know," said Joe. "Frank says he wandered off."

"Wandered off?" asked Chet. "At a time like this?"

"He probably wanted to jump up and down with joy," said Joe, "and was afraid he might accidentally fall into the pit."

"I guess so," said Chet. "Maybe— Hey, did you feel a drop of rain?"

"No," said Frank. "Look up, Chet. The sky's clear blue. No clouds."

"I felt it, too," said Jack. "There's water coming from someplace."

"Water?" said Frank, looking up. "Where would water—? Uh-oh! Look!"

Halfway up the side of the pit, water was trickling out of the opening to the seawater tunnel.

"Oh, that's just great!" said Joe. "The seawater's coming in again. The dam must have broken!"

"Let's grab the rope and get out of here before the water starts coming out for real," said Frank.

"Where *is* the rope?" said George, looking around the pit. "It was hanging right here a minute ago."

Chet looked around in sudden panic. "It's gone!" he cried. "The rope's vanished!"

"Huh?" said Joe. "Where would it go?"

Frank looked up toward the top of the pit. "Right

there," he said, pointing. Dangling high above them, almost at the top of the pit, was the rope they had been using to climb in and out.

"Hey, Professor!" Joe shouted. "Where are you? You've got to throw the rope back down to us before the pit fills up with water again!"

Professor Damien appeared at the mouth of the pit, a grim expression on his face.

"I'm sorry, Joe," he said. "I can't."

"What do you mean, you can't?" Bill demanded. "All you have to do is grab it and toss it down to us. You're not going to let us drown, are you?"

"I'm afraid that's exactly what I'm going to do," Damien said. "Allow you to drown. All of you."

14 Double-Crossed

Frank stared up at the top of the pit. The rope dangled just below where the professor was standing, but Damien didn't pick it up.

"Um, Professor," said Frank. "I must have heard you wrong. I could have sworn you just said that you were going to let us drown."

"That's correct," Damien said bluntly. "I've hammered loose the concrete dam in the cave, reopening the seawater tunnel. The dam had already been weakened by the storm, so it was easy to break. The tide is coming in now. Just a trickle of water is flowing at the moment, but it won't be long before the water will begin pouring into the pit."

"But we can't survive in a pit filled with water!" Joe cried.

"That's true," said the professor. He sighed deeply. "I regret the necessity of doing this. I've enjoyed working with you, especially with you Hardys and Chet."

"Why?" shouted Chet. "Why are you doing this to us?"

"The treasure," said Damien. "I almost wish you hadn't found it. The treasure is more important than anyone's life, yours or mine. No one must know that it's here, not yet, anyway."

"You're not making sense, Professor," said George. "If this treasure's so important, why don't you want anybody to know it's here?"

"The treasure vault you discovered," said Damien, "is one of the greatest archaeological finds of the century. I must keep it out of the hands of people like Vernon Prescott, Barrett Kingsley, and Hurd Applegate."

"I don't get it," said Frank. "What are they going to do to the treasure that's so bad?"

"Sell it to the highest bidder!" Damien exclaimed.

"But they said that they'd go with your decision on what to do with the treasure," said Frank.

"Oh, yes," Damien said bitterly. "I've heard that before. *Now* they claim they want me to decide how the treasure will be disposed of. But when they realize how much it's worth, they'll change their minds.

"On my last expedition," he continued, "we unearthed a perfectly preserved pirate ship that sank in 1699. It was a magnificent find, rich with important artifacts—and what happened to it? The corporation that had financed the dig sold the ship and all its contents to a group of rich collectors, who keep it locked away in a private warehouse. I took the corporation and the collectors to court, trying to regain legal rights to my find, but it did me no good at all!"

"Maybe this time things will be different," Frank said. "Maybe Hurd and Mr. Prescott and Mr. Kingsley will sell or donate it to a museum."

"I can't take that chance," said Damien. "People like that can't see past their own bank accounts."

"But what good will it do to kill us?" said Frank. "It won't get you the treasure."

"Oh, but it will," said Damien. "I'll report that the six of you died in a tragic accident, when you triggered an old pirate trap. Then I'll recommend the pit be closed and the search for the treasure abandoned. As the archaeological expert on this expedition, my word will be heeded.

"Besides," he continued, "our friends Applegate, Prescott, and Kingsley will have their hands full with the legal problems that are sure to come up after your deaths. They'll be sorry they ever heard of Granite Cay. The pit will be filled and the treasure buried again.

"Then, when things have calmed down, I will quietly speak to the directors of several major museums and suggest that there may be important artifacts on this island. I'm sure I'll be able to find someone willing to purchase the island from Mr. Kingsley and to finance a new expedition. I'll be the director of that expedition, of course—and this time I'll make sure the treasure trove of the Uzca falls into proper hands."

"You've really got this worked out," said Chet.

"Wait a minute!" said Frank. "When they drain the pit to get our bodies out, won't they find the treasure chamber and the treasure?"

"They might," Damien said with a nod. "So I'll have to drain the pit myself, using the pump. I'll remove your bodies and fill the pit with dirt until the treasure chamber is covered once again. Then I'll throw your bodies back in the pit, allow it to fill with water again, and then report your deaths."

"Look!" shouted Frank. "The water's starting to flow for real!"

Sure enough, the trickle of water coming through the seawater tunnel was flowing down the wall in a steady current. The floor of the pit was already six inches deep in water.

"The tide is coming in," said Damien. "The pit will fill more and more rapidly, and then we'll have to say goodbye."

"It was you all along, right, Professor?" said Joe.

126

"You're the one who put the board in the tree and the one who cut the rope."

Damien looked puzzled. "No," he said. "You're wrong about that, Joe. I had nothing to do with those things. Why would I? I had no reason to want to hurt you—at least not until you discovered the treasure."

"Then who did?" asked Joe. "Who tried to kill us before *you* tried to kill us?"

"Maybe it *was* these guys," said Chet, looking toward Prescott's workmen.

"Well?" Frank asked. "Was it you? You might as well tell us. It doesn't look like we're getting out of this pit alive."

"We already told you!" snapped Bill. "We didn't have anything to do with it!"

"He's telling the truth," said George. "We gave you kids a hard time, but we didn't want to hurt you. It's a little late for apologies, but I'm sorry we were so rough."

"Me, too," grunted Jack Kruger.

"Yeah, yeah, I'm sorry, too," muttered Bill Drake, after George gently prodded him in the arm.

"Well, for what it's worth, I accept your apologies," said Frank. "And I think Joe and Chet do, too. But then who tried to kill us?"

"I think I can answer that," said a familiar voice from the top of the pit.

Damien's face turned white. He looked up to see a middle-aged man in a knit shirt and expensive designer jeans standing on the opposite side of the pit, a pistol in one hand.

"Barrett Kingsley!" cried Joe.

"One and the same," the man said. "Now, if Professor Damien would like to climb into the pit and join you—I'm going to have the privilege of watching *all* of you die!"

15 Triple-Crossed

Damien stared at Kingsley as the real-estate tycoon pointed his pistol at him across the mouth of the pit.

"What are you doing?" said Damien. "You can't force me into this pit! That would be murder!"

"You're a fine one to talk, Damien," Kingsley said with a chuckle. "I overheard that whole lecture you were giving these gentlemen about how they had to die so that nasty villains like me wouldn't take your treasure away."

He gestured toward the pit. "Now I'm going to lower this rope partway into the pit and you're going to climb down it. I'm afraid you'll have to jump the last few feet. We can't have anybody using this rope to climb back out, can we?"

"I—I can't do that," Damien said, gasping. "I'm too weak. I can't climb down that rope."

"Oh, I think you'll manage," said Kingsley, waving his gun at the archaeologist.

Kingsley bent over and lowered the rope back into the pit. Haltingly, Damien climbed over the edge and into the pit. When he reached the end of the rope, Frank and Joe helped him to the bottom. Then Kingsley quickly pulled the rope back up to the mouth of the pit.

Jack Kruger tapped Damien on the shoulder. "Well, Professor," he said in his rumbling voice, smiling faintly. "Now we're both in the pit."

Damien recoiled.

"Not now, Jack," said Frank. "The professor won't be hurting anybody for the moment, and he may be able to help us out of here. Save your anger for later."

"Well, okay," Kruger grumbled. He backed away but continued to glare at Damien.

"What's this all about, Mr. Kingsley?" asked Joe. "Is this the thanks we get for finding the treasure for you?"

Kingsley smiled and nodded. "Oh, I'm quite grateful, Joe," he said. "I am indeed. But I'm afraid I have no desire to share the treasure with those greedy vultures Applegate and Prescott."

"But you agreed to share it with them," Frank reminded him.

"I was forced into it," said Kingsley with a smile. "Unfortunately, we signed papers, so it won't be easy to get them out of the picture. After your unfortunate deaths, I'll have to convince them the treasure doesn't exist. I can then dig it up in my own good time and sell it quietly on the black market."

Damien's face turned red. "You're unscrupulous, Kingsley! I knew it all along!" Damien's shoulders sagged. "I've lost," he said. "The treasure has fallen into the hands of ignorant fools, just as I feared."

"Hey, Kingsley," Joe called. "Were you the one who put the board in the tree and cut the rope? Have you been hanging around this island all along?"

"That was me, yes," admitted Kingsley. "I've had my boat parked in a secluded cove on the north side of the island, practically since you first arrived. I've watched you all along, except of course during the hurricane. When you found the treasure, I knew it would be necessary to dispose of you."

He smiled at Frank and Joe. "Since you two were clearly the smartest members of the group—with the possible exception of the professor, of course—I thought I should get rid of you first, in case you decided to cause trouble later on. Unfortunately, I did less than a perfect job of it. But it doesn't matter. You'll all be gone soon."

"And you were the one who sent our boat out into the middle of the bay?" asked Frank.

"Right again," said Kingsley. "I didn't think you

would survive the hurricane. But you were more resourceful than I would have guessed."

"How'd you cut the rope with everybody watching?" asked Joe.

"I had to wait until our friend, the professor, had wandered off to the beach and Mr. Kruger was taking a break," said Kingsley. "It took only a minute to make the necessary cut."

"The water's up to my knees," Chet said nervously. "Does it look to you like the water's starting to flow harder?"

"Yeah," said Frank. "It does."

"So you're really going to let us drown?" Joe asked Kingsley.

There was a look of distaste on Kingsley's face. "Oh, no. I think this whole drowning business is too messy. It'll draw attention to the pit. The treasure might be discovered, even if I followed Professor Damien's plan of draining the pit and filling it with dirt. I brought a small tractor with me on my ship, with an earth-moving blade attached. I'm simply going to bulldoze some of this dirt back into the pit, burying you alive. With the pit refilled, it will look as if you simply abandoned the job unfinished, probably to flee the hurricane. When your unmanned boat is found in Barmet Bay, it will be assumed that you were washed overboard by the storm. The police will drag the bay for your bodies,

132

but they won't find you. You'll be written off as victims of the storm."

"If you don't want us to drown," Frank said, pointing at the flood pouring down the wall, "then you'd better plug up that tunnel real soon."

"Oh, yes," said Kingsley. "I've got some caulking materials that should do the job. I'll be back in a moment."

"Don't hurry back on our account," said Joe, as Kingsley disappeared from view.

"What do we do now?" asked Frank. "He'll be gone for a few minutes. It's our only chance to get away."

"There's not much we can do," said Chet. "The rope ladder's out of reach, and this pit's too slippery to climb."

"May I ask a favor?" said Damien. "Since we're all about to die anyway?"

"Shut up," snapped Bill. "After you tried to kill us, I'm not doing you any favors."

"Please," begged Damien. "I'd just like to see the treasure, to touch it, before I die."

"Hah!" said Bill Drake. "You aren't going anywhere near it!"

"What's the difference?" said Joe. "He's stuck in here, too. He might as well get to see the treasure before Kingsley buries us alive."

"Okay, Professor," said Frank. "You'll need a boost. Give me a hand, Joe."

133

Together they lifted the professor through the narrow hole and into the treasure chamber. Joe then handed him the battery-operated lantern.

"Now let's figure out how to get out of here," said Frank. "Maybe if we formed a kind of human pyramid."

"A human pyramid?" said Joe. "More like a human ladder! It must be twenty-five feet to the top of the pit. It'd take five guys on each other's shoulders to reach the top—and the guy on the bottom would be squashed flat by the weight of everybody on top!"

"*I'll* stand on the bottom," offered Jack Kruger.

Joe stared at Kruger's wide shoulders and reconsidered. "Well, maybe *you* wouldn't be squashed."

"Chet can stand on top of Kruger," said Frank, "I can stand on top of Chet, Bill can stand on top of me, and you can stand on top of Bill. I think we can do it."

"I think you're crazy," said Joe. "We'll kill ourselves trying!"

"I hate to remind you," said George, "but Kingsley's going to kill us if we don't get out of here."

"Good point," said Joe. "Okay, Chet, you climb onto Jack's shoulders."

Kruger grabbed Chet's arms in his huge hands and lifted the stocky teen off the ground. Chet took a tight grip on Kruger's shoulders and pulled himself onto them, awkwardly rising to a standing position.

"Okay," said Frank. "That takes us nearly halfway there."

"You're next," said Joe. "You can just— Uh-oh!"

"What?" asked Frank. "Is something wrong?"

"Yeah," said Joe, pointing to the seawater tunnel. "The water's stopping."

"What's wrong with that?" asked Chet. "You don't want to drown, do you?"

"It means Kingsley's already sealed the tunnel," said Joe. "I didn't think he could work that fast. If he catches us trying to climb out of here, he might do something desperate."

"Like plugging us full of bullets?" said Frank.

"Something like that, yeah," replied Joe.

"I think I hear somebody coming," Chet said.

"Get down!" said Joe. "Don't let Kingsley see you on Jack's shoulders!"

Chet jumped back to the ground. "What are we going to do, then?" he asked.

"We may get another chance," said Frank. "He's got to go for the earth mover, right? We'll just move fast when he does."

Kingsley reappeared above them. "You'll be happy to know," he said, "that you're not going to drown. I've sealed the tunnel."

"Thanks," said Frank. "We really appreciate your efforts to make things nicer for us down here."

135

"Sarcasm doesn't become you, Frank," said Kingsley. He smiled menacingly at the group. "Don't go away. I'll be right back."

As soon as Kingsley moved out of view, Chet started to climb onto Kruger's shoulders again. Then suddenly, Professor Damien poked his head out of the treasure chamber and started shouting.

"Kingsley!" he yelled. "Come back here! I've got something to tell you!"

"Keep it down!" Joe said urgently. "Can't you see we're trying to get out of here! We don't *want* Kingsley to come back!"

Kingsley reappeared at the mouth of the pit. "What is it, Damien? What are you making all that noise about?"

"I've got news for you, Kingsley!" the professor shouted. "Very bad news!"

"What in the world are you talking about?" Kingsley snapped.

"Here's your treasure, Kingsley!" cried Damien, holding a necklace of glittering jewels in his outstretched hand. "I've just been examining it, and guess what?"

He squeezed his hand into a fist and the jewels crumbled into a powder, raining tiny shards of dust down to the floor of the pit.

"They're paste!" Damien shouted. "They're phony! The whole treasure trove of the Uzca is a fake!"

16 The Greatest Treasure of All

Kingsley's eyes widened in horror.

"No!" he shouted. "It's a trick! You're lying!"

"It's no trick, Kingsley," Damien replied bitterly. "The jewelry is paste, and the gold bars are painted lead. The jade statues and gold weapons are probably fakes, too. This treasure isn't worth killing for."

"You can't fool me!" said Kingsley. "You're just lying to save your worthless hide. I'm not going to fall for it. You'll all be dead as soon as I get back here with the tractor." Scowling, Kingsley disappeared from view.

"Let's move!" said Frank. "Chet, get back on Jack's shoulders. We have to reach the mouth of the pit before Kingsley gets back!"

"What are we going to do then?" Joe asked. "Remember, Kingsley's got a gun."

"We'll worry about that when we get out of here," said Frank.

Chet hastily mounted Kruger's shoulders, then Frank climbed onto Kruger's massive back, and from there onto Chet's shoulders.

Then Bill Drake climbed over Kruger, Chet, and finally Frank. By the time he was on Frank's shoulders, the entire human ladder was beginning to shake back and forth wildly.

"Grab the wall, everybody!" yelled Joe. "Keep your balance. I've got to climb over you."

"Be careful," said Frank. "It's a long fall if you don't make it!"

"Ouch!" said Chet. "You guys must weigh a ton! Hurry up!"

"I'm almost there," said Joe, boosting himself onto Bill Drake's shoulders. "Just give me a second."

"Watch your foot, Hardy," said Bill. "You almost kicked me in the eye."

"Sorry," said Joe. "I—" The roar of heavy machinery suddenly started up in the distance. "Uh-oh. Sounds like Kingsley and his tractor."

"Better get moving," said Frank.

"Here I go," said Joe, rising to his feet on Bill's shoulders. He put out his arms, grasped the edge of

the pit, and pulled himself up. The rope was barely
dangling over the edge. Joe tossed it into the pit,
where the other members of the human ladder
scrambled to grab hold of it.

"Move it, guys," urged Joe. "I hear Kingsley
getting closer."

One by one, the others climbed up the rope and
clambered over the edge of the pit. As the last of
the treasure hunters emerged, a small tractor came
roaring around the corner from the beach and into
the clearing. Barrett Kingsley, seated at the wheel,
stopped the tractor and stared at the treasure pit in
astonishment.

"You!" he cried when he saw the group assem-
bled around the pit. "How did you get out of
there?"

"Sorry, Kingsley," said Joe. "Wish we could stick
around for the rest of your show, but we've got to
run."

"Get back in there!" yelled Kingsley, jumping off
the tractor and running across the clearing, waving
his gun as he ran.

"We'd better get out of here," yelled Joe.

"I'm with you," said Frank.

"But where to?" said Chet.

"Into the woods," said Joe. "I've got an idea."

Joe darted into the woods, Frank and Chet close
behind him. Kingsley fired at them as he ran, the
bullets whizzing past them into the trees.

"This way," said Joe, pointing deeper into the forest. "Just follow me."

Frank could hear the others rushing into the woods on all sides, scrambling to put a few dozen trees between themselves and Kingsley's bullets. Frank and Chet zigzagged through the woods after Joe. Behind them they could hear Kingsley gasping for breath as he pursued them. The real-estate developer must be close behind.

"I sure hope you've got a plan," Frank told his brother.

"Trust me," said Joe with a smile. "We've gone far enough into the woods now. Just stop and let Kingsley come and get us."

"Huh?" said Chet, staring at his friend in astonishment. Joe stopped running and turned around, standing boldly between two trees. He glanced at the thick mud in front of them and grinned broadly. Frank turned to see Kingsley running after them in hot pursuit. Then, startled by the change in Joe's behavior, the real-estate tycoon slowed and approached more cautiously, his gun held high.

"I changed my mind," Joe said in a casual tone. "I got tired of running."

"What are you up to?" Kingsley said, approaching slowly. "Is this a trick?"

"Trick?" said Joe, opening his eyes wide. "What kind of trick could it be? Come here and get us, and

140

we'll come back to the treasure pit. You have the gun, after all."

"All right," said Kingsley. "I will."

He took a step forward into a wide clearing between trees, pointing his gun at Joe.

Suddenly the ground dropped out from under him. With a shout, he sank into the quicksand that had trapped Joe two days earlier.

"Hey!" yelled Kingsley. "What in the world—?" He looked down in terror. "Get me out of here!" he shouted, waving his gun in the air. "Help me! I'm sinking!"

Chet kept going, but the Hardys dodged behind a pair of trees, in case Kingsley started shooting again.

"Throw us the gun, Kingsley," shouted Frank. "The more you wave it around, the faster you'll sink."

"Are you ready to surrender?" Joe shouted.

"No," yelled Kingsley. Then he looked down at the quicksand, which was nearly up to his elbows. "I mean, yes! Just get me out of this stuff! Please!"

"Throw us the gun, and we'll help you out," said Joe.

Kingsley threw the gun onto the ground. Joe picked it up, and Frank gave Kingsley the same instructions Professor Damien had given Joe two days before. Moments later, Frank and Joe were pulling Kingsley out of the quicksand.

Chet appeared at the edge of the woods. "Hey, you guys!" he yelled. "There's a boat here! I think we're being rescued!"

"It's about time," said Joe. "Come on, Kingsley. We're taking you back to Bayport."

The Hardys and Chet met up with the three workmen on their way out of the woods. When they reached the beach, they saw a Coast Guard cruiser parked just offshore. A small party had disembarked from the boat, including three Coast Guard officers, Hurd Applegate, Vernon Prescott, and Fenton Hardy, Joe and Frank's father.

"Boy, are we glad to see you guys!" said Frank, as their rescuers waded onto the beach.

"Not half as glad as I am to see you," announced Fenton Hardy. "We found your boat in the middle of the bay earlier this afternoon. We were afraid you had all drowned."

"We almost did drown," said Joe, "a couple of times. But not in the storm."

"What do you mean?" asked Hurd Applegate.

"We'll tell you all about it later, Mr. Applegate," said Frank. He turned to the Coast Guard officer. "We've got a couple of prisoners for you. Attempted murder. Barrett Kingsley here tried to kill all seven of us."

After hasty explanations, Kingsley was handcuffed and taken back to the cruiser. The three

142

workmen boarded the boat, too. Professor Damien, though, was nowhere to be found.

Chet snapped his fingers. "We left him at the bottom of the pit. He's probably still looking at the treasure."

"He probably still can't believe it's fake," said Joe.

"Come on," Frank said to the others. "We'll take you to him. I hope you don't mind doing a little climbing."

One by one, Frank, Joe, Chet, Fenton Hardy, Vernon Prescott, and two of the Coast Guard officers lowered themselves down the rope and into the treasure pit. Inside the treasure chamber, they found Professor Rupert Damien sitting next to the battery-operated lantern, looking sadly at his "treasure."

"I can't believe it," he said with a moan. "None of it is real. How could such a thing have happened?"

"What are you talking about?" said Vernon Prescott. "Not real? You mean my treasure's a phony?"

"That's exactly what I mean," said Damien. "Henry Dafoe must have intended this as a practical joke. He must have laughed at the thought of treasure hunters coming after his treasure and finding only paste jewels and lead gold."

"I don't buy it," said Frank. "Henry Dafoe

doesn't sound like the kind of guy who would have done all this just for a few laughs. I think there's a real treasure down here somewhere."

"But where?" said Damien. "We've looked all over."

"Maybe not," said Frank. "Maybe we haven't looked quite far enough."

"Yeah," said Joe. "This could be just another of Dafoe's little tricks, like the empty chest."

"Dafoe dug down twenty feet," said Frank. "Then he went sideways. Where would he go next?"

"Up?" said Joe.

"Let's find out," said Frank. "Give me that lantern, Professor."

Frank took the lantern from Damien and held it up to the ceiling of the chamber. Then he began to study the color of the dirt over their heads.

"Look," he said finally. "The dirt's a little darker here, just like it was on the wall of the treasure chamber. Hand me a shovel, Joe."

Joe did as his brother asked. Frank began poking at the ceiling of the chamber with the shovel, knocking chunks of dirt to the floor.

"Be careful, Frank," warned Fenton Hardy. "You might cause a cave-in. There's a great deal of earth above us here."

"I'll take it easy, Dad," said Frank. "I—"

Suddenly the dirt overhead started to move, and

a large chunk fell out of the ceiling and onto the floor, just missing Frank's head. When the dust settled, they saw what had fallen out of the hole. It was a heavy object about three feet long and two feet tall.

"It's a chest!" exclaimed Joe. "A wooden chest, just like the one we found in the treasure pit."

"Amazing," said Damien.

Frank stooped beside the chest and cleared the centuries-old dirt off it. As before, the initials *HD* were carved on one side. Chet retrieved the drill from the pit, and Frank used it to break open the lock.

He opened the chest with shaking hands and stared inside.

There was only one thing in the chest. His heart in his throat, Frank reached inside and pulled it out.

It was an emerald, the largest he had ever seen and incredibly beautiful.

"Is it—is it real, Professor?" asked Frank. "Or is it another fake?"

Damien took the emerald from Frank and examined it carefully. "It's real," he said finally. "Absolutely real."

Joe stared at it with wide eyes. "Then it must be—"

"—the Green Star of the Amazon," finished Damien. "It exists. It really exists!"

"So the legend was true," said Frank. "The treasure trove of the Uzca was real, and this was its greatest treasure."

"I guess old Henry Dafoe wasn't turned into a human sacrifice after all," said Chet.

Vernon Prescott's eyes glistened. "That little baby ought to be worth a fortune!" he said. "I'm going to be rich!"

"You already are rich," Frank pointed out. "You'll just be richer."

"Not necessarily," said Fenton Hardy. "Barrett Kingsley owns the island on which this treasure was found, and he's currently under arrest. The ownership of this stone is going to be tied up legally for some years to come."

"What?" said Prescott. "That's ridiculous! One third of this stone is mine."

"Maybe," said Fenton. "If you're willing to wait awhile."

"I've got an idea," Joe said suddenly. "Professor Damien said the stone belonged to the Uzca, who lived in what's now Costa de Oro. But Henry Dafoe apparently stole it from them. So wouldn't this stone be the property of the people of Costa de Oro?"

"Perhaps," said Fenton Hardy. "But the emerald is so old it might be difficult to legally prove who really owns it."

"Well," said Joe, "I was thinking it might make

things a lot easier—legally speaking—if Hurd Applegate, Vernon Prescott, and Barrett Kingsley make a gift of the Green Star to the people of Costa de Oro. It's part of their cultural heritage, after all, and it might avoid some thorny legal problems about the ownership of the stone."

"True," Fenton said, nodding. "It just might."

"What?" barked Vernon Prescott. "Give up the stone? Are you crazy?"

"Chances are, you'd spend a lot less time in court deciding who actually owns the stone," Fenton said pointedly.

"Well," grumbled Prescott, "maybe I'll think about it."

"Good idea," said Fenton Hardy. "We'll talk to Hurd Applegate about it when we get out of here."

"Wait," said Rupert Damien as the others turned to leave. "May I hold the stone a minute longer?"

"I guess so," said Frank, handing it to him. "Just don't try to steal it."

"I don't think I'm in a position to do that," Damien said dryly, as he stared intently at the jewel. "I just wanted to enjoy the fruits of my labors, if only for a moment. I suspect I won't be allowed to do much archaeology where I'm going."

"In prison?" said Joe. "No, I guess you won't."

"But it's nice to know that there really was a treasure," Damien said with a sigh. "This would have been the greatest discovery of my career."

"It still is," said Frank. "I'm sure you'll get the credit for it."

"Yes," admitted Damien. "There is that."

One by one the group made its way back up to the top of the pit. Damien was handcuffed and led on board the cruiser, then the others followed.

"Dinner's still at my place," said Chet.

"Great," said Joe, standing at the railing as the ship pulled into Barmet Bay. "I'm starving."

"Me, too," said Frank. "We never had lunch."

"Treasure hunting sure is hungry work," said Chet.

"For you," said Joe, "everything is hungry work."

"Hey, that's true," said Chet. "I hadn't thought of it that way. Let's go eat!"

"So, Mr. Applegate," said Joe, staring out the window of Hurd Applegate's condominium high atop Tower Mansion. "I'm glad to hear that you and Vernon Prescott agreed to donate that emerald to the people of Costa de Oro."

"Yes," agreed Chet, who was sitting on the windowsill. "And that picture in *Profile* magazine of you and Vernon Prescott handing the stone to the president of Costa de Oro was pretty nice, too."

"So why did you ask us to come up here, Mr. Applegate?" asked Frank. "To see your condo again? It's looking really great. I have to admit that

George, Bill, and Jack did one terrific job of putting the place together."

"That's true," said Hurd, gazing around at the freshly painted walls and the brand-new door that led into what was once his father's secret workshop. "Even if they are a trio of ruffians."

"The apartment will look even better when you get some new furniture," said Joe, glancing around. "This stuff is pretty, well, *antique*-looking."

"That's not what I called you about," said Hurd, waving aside Joe's comment. "I was doing some more rummaging in my father's papers and I came across *this.*"

He pulled a yellowing sheet of paper out of his coat pocket and held it out for Frank, Joe, and Chet to look at. Written across the top was the word *Deed.* Underneath was a lot of spidery handwriting and what looked to be several signatures.

"What is it?" Joe asked.

"It's a deed that belonged to my father," Hurd explained. "It's for a silver mine in the middle of Arizona, which apparently I have inherited."

"Well, congratulations, Mr. Applegate!" said Frank. "That's terrific! That should take some of the sting out of giving away the treasure of the Uzca."

"There's only one problem," said Hurd. "It seems that no one is quite sure where the mine is. It's somewhere at the bottom of a vast natural cavern. I'm told it can be reached only by crossing a large underground lake and penetrating a tunnel that leads far below the earth. No one has been down there in years. How my father ended up with such a thing, I have no idea."

Joe and Frank exchanged glances. "Exactly why did you call us?" Joe asked.

"I'll be needing someone to locate the mine," Hurd Applegate said, "and I was hoping you boys . . ."

"Uh, I think I just remembered that our parents and Aunt Gertrude were expecting us home early this evening for a family party," said Frank. "Chet's invited, too. We really have to be going."

"Right, Mr. Applegate," said Joe. "It was nice seeing your condo and all. We really hope you find somebody to help you locate your silver mine. We were just on our way out."

"Hey," said Chet. "This sounds kind of neat. I've always wanted to see the inside of a silver mine."

"No, you haven't, Chet," said Joe, leading his friend out of the small apartment by the collar of his shirt.

"But I had intended to ask you—" said Hurd.

"Thanks but no thanks," said Frank. "One treasure hunt per lifetime is enough for anybody. I've had mine and so have Joe and Chet."

"Goodbye, Mr. Applegate," cried Frank and Joe simultaneously. With a laugh, they led Chet back down the stairs of Tower Mansion and outside to the Hardy van.

"I just want to get back to my normal, dull, everyday life," Frank said as he slid into the driver's seat.

"Yeah, me, too," said Joe. He sat quietly for a moment. Then he looked at his brother. "At least, until something better comes along. You know, like another case?"

"Absolutely," Frank replied with a grin.

THE HARDY BOYS® SERIES By Franklin W. Dixon